SPINDELKIN

JEAN DAVIS

ISBN-13:   (print) 979-8-9850814-2-8
             (ebook) 979-8-9850814-3-5

First Edition: May 2022

Also by Jean Davis

Destiny Pills & Space Wizards
Sahmara
A Broken Race
The Last God
Dreams of Stars and Lies
Not Another Bard's Tale
Everyone Dies
Frayed

The Narvan
One Shot at the Sphinx
Trust
The Minor Years
Chain of Gray
Bound In Blue
Seeker
Tears of the Tyrant

1

POISON

eep within the shining city of Katra, between the shimmering ocean shores to the east and the endless forest to the west, Amira lay in her bed. She'd never seen the oceans or the forest, but the endless stream of maids over the years had told her about them. Her father had shown her maps. Her mother didn't approve of any of that. Amira needed to focus on getting well and that was all she should concern herself with.

In all her eleven years, she'd heard about the wonders of Katra, the city that glowed in splendor even at night. From her windowless room, she couldn't see the moon or the city or the bustling crowds of people in their beautiful clothes walking the streets. The only people that came to see her were her mother and father and the maid. There had been a little girl long ago, someone to play with, to pass the hours with stories and laughter, but then, like so many maids, one day she was gone.

When Amira was younger she would ask where

people went, and why they left, but Mother would just say, "They have other chores. They have their own children to attend to. We'll get by without them."

The burnt-down candle on the table beside her bed told Amira it was morning. Mother would be here soon.

With a trembling arm, she pushed herself off the thick mattress and swung her thin legs over the edge of the bed. Once her slippered feet touched the floor, she waited a moment for the dizziness to go away before making use of the chamber pot and then washing her hands and face in the basin on the stand across the room. She was standing there, catching her breath, when the maid unlocked the door and came in.

"Good morning, mistress. Did you sleep well?" asked the plump sun-kissed woman no taller than Amira.

"Yes." She always said yes. It was easier than telling the truth.

"Very good, mistress. Let's get you dressed." She opened the wardrobe and smiled widely. "Blue or green today?"

"Blue." Not that it mattered, but having an answer made the maids happy.

"You look lovely in blue, I'm sure. Here now, let me help you."

Amira didn't have a choice. It had been two years since she'd had the strength to dress herself. Maybe it was the fault of the dresses her mother chose. As Amira grew older, the dresses grew more intricate, bigger, fuller, and had so many layers. Sometimes it seemed like the skirts would swallow her whole when she sat on her bed.

After the maid cinched the last cord, she stood back. "There now, you do look lovely. Let's get to work on your hair. The Queen will be here shortly."

Amira sat on the stool, lost in her sea of blue skirts while the maid combed out the night tangles. She clasped her hands together on her lap to hide how much they shook. Even the thought of walking across the room in the heavy dress and getting herself back up onto the bed made her exhausted.

"You've got the finest skin I've ever seen," said the maid. "Flawless. Envy of all the women in Katra, I'd say. We just need to get you well. I'm sure your parents will have a fine prince waiting for you one day soon."

Amira nodded. Mother had never mentioned a prince or marriage or anything of the like. It was as though her mother knew the truth of things just as Amira did. She wasn't going to get better. There would be no grand wedding, no glorious feast, no music, no leaving this room to move to a far-off kingdom.

The maid sang softly as she brushed Amira's hair. She closed her eyes and enjoyed the song, losing herself in the long, slow brush strokes.

"Mistress?"

The maid's panicked voice brought Amira awake with a start.

She tumbled off the stool and landed in a puddle of skirts.

"Oh heavens!" The maid scrambled to get to Amira

without stepping on the dress, reaching out to grab Amira's hands and trying to pull her to her feet.

The queen walked in. "What are you doing on the floor? Get her up at once!"

The maid darted forward and hoisted Amira onto her feet. Fabric tore loudly as she did so.

The maid went stiff and bit her lip.

"Get out!" Mother grabbed the maid's arm and yanked her out of the room. The wooden door closed behind both of them, muting Mother's angry words.

When she returned, she closed the door behind her and fluffed her skirts for a moment, smoothing her dress over the large mound of her belly. "Are you hurt?"

Amira's wrist stung and her hip ached where she'd landed, but if she said no, the maid might be allowed to return. "No, Mother. I fell off the stool, it wasn't her fault."

"She didn't catch you," Mother said tightly. "You should change your dress. It's torn."

Though she always did her best to be polite and do as her mother asked, the thought of taking off the dress and putting on another was too much. "It's fine, Mother. No one sees me but you."

"Your father might."

"He hasn't come to see me in weeks." And she missed him. He often sat and played games with her and told her some of what was going on throughout Katra. He made her room feel a little less small.

"He's been busy. We're all busy, Amira. We do our

best to spend time with you."

"Yes, Mother." She started toward the bed, trying to hide the limp from the pain in her hip. Thankfully, the skirts did her a favor for once. If only she could just stay in her nightdress all the time she'd be far more comfortable. But Mother had declared she would dress as befitting her station.

Mother's dress was just as fine. Today, blue jewels adorned her slender neck. Two golden rings with blue stones clinked together as she patted the towering mound of dark curls piled atop her head. Candlelight twinkled on the tiny jeweled pins that held her hair in place. Amira hoped to be as beautiful as Mother one day, but she'd have to be healthy for that. She was too tired, too pale, too small. Mother had explained that Amira's illness had leeched the color from her body along with her strength.

Mother urged Amira toward the bed with an impatient wave.

When she was younger, she'd thought the step beside her bed was there because she was too little to get up on her own. She'd asked to have it removed several times, but it never went away. More recently, she was grateful it was still there. Amira took a deep breath and hoisted her mighty girth of skirts onto the bed. On any other day, the maid would have put the bedcovers back to order before Amira sat down, but that hadn't happened this morning.

Mother scowled at the mess on the bed, but the

dress covered most of it and in the end, she merely shook her head and let out a loud sigh. "Let's get started, shall we?"

Amira sat forward while her mother piled pillows behind her and then leaned back onto the fluffy cloud. She liked to think of them as a cloud so she could be floating high above Katra, looking down on the green fields and merry-colored homes.

The prick in her arm barely registered anymore. Mother used a different location each day, allowing the wounds to heal. Next came the clear tube, one end dangling into a clean, clear jar on the bedside table. It only took a moment for the golden glow to light the tube and begin to drip into the jar.

The poison.

Venom remained in her body, and no matter how much of it was drained away, there was always more. She'd been cursed when she was an infant, but no one knew who had done the horrible deed.

The treatments used to only last the morning and by lunch, she could get out of bed to play. But as she grew older, the treatments took longer. Now they lasted until supper and even after they were done, she had no desire to get out of bed, to walk, to play, to do much of anything but perhaps talk a little. If there was anyone to talk to.

"Will I ever leave this room?" She knew better than to expect a different answer than the one Mother always gave, but every now and again, desperation prodded her to ask.

Mother patted Amira's other arm. "Time will tell. Rest now, you're so pale today."

Time always kept its mouth shut.

"Yes, Mother."

She tried not to notice how awkward it was for her mother to now go about her usual tasks, arranging Amira's dress just so and putting the brush and cloth in order by the basin. It wouldn't be long before she'd know if she would have a brother or sister. Mother said it was bad luck to talk about the unborn, so Amira did her best to be patient and keep her questions to herself.

Mother's stomach had been this big twice before but she'd never brought a baby to see Amira. When she'd asked her maids about it, they'd been sad and mumbled words about the pregnancy not working out. Amira prayed this one would. She dearly wanted a brother or sister to visit her, someone healthy to make Mother happy.

She settled for asking, "Are you well, Mother?"

"Well enough. I'll be back to check on you before midday."

Amira watched her leave, closing the door behind her. It was almost a game to see if she could catch a glimpse of the guard or whomever it was outside her door, but she never could.

A fresh candle lit her bedside while another illuminated the stand and stool. Tiny facets in the stone floor glittered in the light of the flame. She'd memorized near every stitch in the tapestry on the wall near the foot of her bed, and fantasized that there was a hidden door behind it that someone might use someday. As long as they were friendly, she would have welcomed the company. Any company, really.

The bouquet of red and pink flowers the maid had brought two days ago was beginning to wilt and the lovely scent had faded away. She'd worn this dress many times, leaving nothing new to explore there either. She began to pick at her nails. Mother wouldn't approve of nibbled nails or bloody fingers. She slid her hands under her legs and closed her eyes.

In the darkness, she could imagine the sounds of the stone, of the walls, the world outside. She could hear people talking, the tones of their voices, even if not their words. She left the castle, floating on the wind.

The song the maid had sung drifted in and out of her memory, playing over and over as butterflies danced on hillsides covered in flowers of all colors. She could run through them, feel their silky petals on her fingers, and inhale the sweet scent of them all. Birds flitted overhead, singing merrily. She stopped there, spinning slowly, arms outstretched, face to the warm sun. Amira laughed. This was one of her favorite places to be. She spent the morning there until a gentle shake brought her back to the tired body on the bed in the candlelit room.

"You need to eat." Mother settled a tray on Amira's lap. "Keep your strength up."

Amira sipped the creamy broth and picked tasty

bits off the slice of warm buttery bread. After she'd eaten, she did feel a little stronger.

"Very good." Mother picked up the tray. "Drink your water."

While Amira drained the cup, Mother switched out the jar, nearly full of golden poison, for a new empty one. She put a cork in the bottle and picked it up, taking the empty tray in her other hand. Rather than head for the door as she usually did, she paused, caressing the bottle of poison. "Your father would like to see you, if you're up for a visit?"

Amira's heart raced at the thought of a break in the monotony. "Oh yes, I'm feeling better than this morning. I would like that very much."

"I've told him not to stay too long. You need to rest and he has work to do."

"Yes, Mother." But he was coming to visit. It didn't matter how long he stayed.

After Mother had left, Amira smoothed the bedcovers that were visible around her dress and then arranged her skirt into neat folds where the tray had flattened the satin fabric. She'd run out of things to fuss with hours before Father brightened her door.

"You came," she announced as he entered the room. His arms were empty and his normally strong and straight shoulders were hunched. "You didn't bring any games today? What's wrong?"

Father's shoes scraped along the stone, his steps halting. "Your mother..."

Amira's throat went dry. "Is she not well? She was here at midday."

"She hasn't been well for a long time." He came to stand on the far side of the bed, gazing at the thin layer of gold at the bottom of the jar on the bedside table.

His voice was thick when he asked, "How are you feeling?"

"Tired. Always tired. I'm sorry, Father, I don't think I'm ever going to get better."

He shook his head of long dark hair. His thick beard rustled over the brocade of his overcoat. "Not here, no."

"Not here? Is there somewhere else? Have you found someone who can help me?"

Mother had been very adamant against having doctors visit. She called them charlatans, wanting gold and offering nothing but lies.

"Yes, elsewhere, but I don't know if we can get you there in time. Or at all."

"Is it far away?" Even if she might not make the journey, it was worth trying if only to see something other than this room before she passed on to the next world. Maybe she could see the flower field with her own eyes just once.

"Yes and no."

He wasn't making much sense. How was he going to help her if he didn't seem to know the answers?

"The maps we used to use...can you show me where I'd have to go?"

Father glanced at the door and clasped his hands

together. "I don't think that's a good idea." He put on a stiff smile and sat down beside her, his back to the jar. "I'm sorry I haven't been to see you. It's hard."

Amira nodded. "Mother said you were busy."

"It's not that." He stared at his hands. "I don't like to see you like this, so ill, so tired. Remember when you were younger, when you could run around the room and we'd play games?"

"Yes, of course. I miss playing games with you."

"That wasn't as hard. You were tired, but not like this. I wish you could go outside, that you could have friends. This was never the life I wanted for you."

She'd never seen Father cry before, but there they were, tears on his cheeks, dripping down to get lost in his beard.

"Don't cry, Father. You're making me sad. This isn't your fault."

"I'm sorry." He wiped at his face. "I wish I could have stopped it. I should have."

"How could you? You said so yourself. I was cursed. Unless you know who did this to me, I don't think there's any other way to stop a curse."

"I should have tried harder to stop her. We had an agreement, and she's kept to it, but this room and fine dresses do not make up for what's been done. My dear Amira, I'm so sorry. Please forgive me. I don't think I can bear to see you again."

He leaned over to kiss her cheek, the rough wet hairs of his beard scraped against her face, but she didn't mind at all.

"Don't leave me here alone. Send the maid back, someone, anyone. I don't want to be alone anymore."

He stood up, causing the bed to dip as he did so. She rocked to one side and then the other until the mattress settled. "You'll be getting a new maid."

"Not another new one." She sighed. "I liked the last one."

"I know. You like them all. You're such a kind soul." He kissed her cheek and then stepped away. His voice shook as he said, "Goodbye Amira." Then he bolted out the door. The lock clicked into place.

2

LILY

The new maid brought supper.

"Where's my mother?" Amira asked, thinking it was very unlike Mother to miss bringing her a meal. "Is she unwell?"

"I'm not privy to the health of the queen, mistress. I'm sure she'll be to see you when she can. Please eat."

"I'm not hungry." She'd been crying since Father left. Why would Mother send him to see her only to say he wouldn't be back. He couldn't have been truthful about that, could he?

"The jar needs changing. My mother must do it," Amira said with all the authority she could muster.

"I'm not to touch the jar, mistress. Can you take care of it?"

She never had. She'd never had to. Mother had been there to do it. But she knew how. She'd watched Mother change it a thousand times. Trying herself would be better than watching the poison overflow onto the floor. It would make anyone who touched it sick. She'd seen that once. One of the maids had thought to clean up a drop that had spilled onto the table beside the jar. The single golden droplet had seeped into her apron and smeared onto her finger. Down on the stones she went, her whole body convulsing. White bubbles had foamed from her mouth a moment later. Amira's scream had alerted the guard outside, but he only shouted for the queen, who came running in a short while later. The maid had been removed. Amira had never seen her again. Mother wouldn't speak of it. Amira didn't know if the maid had survived.

If one drop of poison in her veins could do that to a person, she didn't want to know what would happen if there was a large spill. "Yes, I suppose I can."

"Sorry to ask that of you, mistress. I understand you're ill."

"Help me up." Amira held out her hand to the tall, dark-skinned woman with greying hair.

The maid hesitated. "Am I allowed to touch you?"

"Yes. Please, this dress is so heavy and I'm so tired." All she'd done was sit in the bed all day but she could barely keep her eyes open. She'd felt better when Father had first arrived, but he'd taken all her energy with him when he'd left.

The maid helped her to the side of the bed. The room spun. She'd never had to pull the needle out on her own and the thought of doing so made her stomach twist and tumble. With her eyes pressed closed, she carefully pulled the needle from her arm.

Once that was done, she kept the tube up high and held onto the maid's hand until she got her footing. The jar was only three steps away, yet it took her six shuffling steps to get there. Her feet were so heavy and they refused to move like they should have.

"You're almost there. Just put the cork in now, mistress," urged the maid.

Amira let go of the maid to grasp the edge of the nightstand. She reached for the cork. It rolled away from her fingers as though it were playing a game of tag. With a hollow thump, it landed on the floor and rolled under her bed.

"Will you find that, please?" Amira held herself up on the nightstand, keeping the end of the tube aloft, while the maid got to her hands and knees.

There on the ground, Amira spotted a tiny drop of the poison. Its golden glimmer held her rapt attention.

If she said nothing, if the maid should touch it and fall ill, Amira would have cause to call for the guard at her door. If Mother was also ill, the guard might come in. She might finally have someone other than a maid or her parents to talk to. If she was lucky, they might leave the door open to see to the maid and she could peek out into the hall. She might even run down it and search for Father so she could see him again.

The maid crawled closer to the drop of poison. Amira clutched the table. She couldn't let the maid suffer, no matter how much she might want to get out of her room. "Stop, don't touch that!"

The woman froze. She turned slowly and spotted the golden droplet. "Surely you have saved me, mistress. I was told what happened to the last maid who was foolish enough to touch it."

"Do you know what happened to her?" Amira ventured to ask.

The maid found the cork and carefully got to her feet. "It is said she lives out her days in the dungeon."

"The dungeon, why?"

"It's not my place to say, mistress, but I have no wish to join her." She handed the cork to Amira. "Best take care of that before there are more spills."

Amira put the cork in the bottle. She set the tube and needle on the nightstand table beside it.

"You should eat." The maid nodded toward the tray on the bed.

"I said, I'm not hungry. Help me undress. I will sleep now."

The maid scowled but she obeyed. Once Amira was free of the dress, she felt a bit better, lighter. She settled back on her pillows and closed her eyes, waiting for the maid to leave.

She'd hadn't truly intended to sleep, but when she again opened her eyes, she was alone and the candles had burned out. Yet, the room wasn't dark. The jar of poison emitted a faint, golden glow. She watched the shimmering light and waited for the maid for what seemed like a very long time.

"Mistress?"

"I'm here." Where else would she be? "Is something wrong?"

"The queen has sent me for the jar." The maid entered with her a little candle. "The king has bade me not to deliver the jar to the queen."

Father didn't want Mother to have the poison? He'd never taken much interest in her treatment before, but he did say that she'd be getting a new maid.

"Did my father send you to be my maid?"

The maid nodded, glancing nervously at the door behind her. "My name is Jancy. The king asked me to get you out of the castle so that you might get the help you need, but I don't know if I can."

Amira's heart beat faster. She could think of nothing she'd like more than to see the world outside her room. But why couldn't Father get her out of the castle? Surely the king could do more than a simple maid.

"Where is the queen?" Amira asked.

"Whispers say your brother has come early. The queen is abed."

A brother? Amira grinned. "Is he well?"

"I do not know, mistress."

"Leave me the candle and go find out." She shooed the maid out the door. If her brother was here at last, she couldn't leave the castle now.

"Yes, mistress." Jancy left the candle on the stand by the basin and hurried out. The door clicked behind her.

Mother had waited for another child for so long. If there was anything Amira could do to help, she would. It was the least she could do. Mother had spent so much time taking care of her.

In her excitement, Amira decided she'd try to get dressed on her own. She slid out of bed and off the stool onto the floor. The cold stone sent a shock through her body, but not nearly as much as when the candlelight caught on the white lilies perched upon thick stalks surrounded by lush leaves. They grew from a crack that hadn't been there the day before. She glanced at the nightstand beside her bed where the jar, needle, and tube still sat.

Amira gasped. The lilies stood right where the drop of poison had fallen.

3

A New Friend

How was this possible? A flower growing from stone? Amira knelt beside the lilies and inhaled their sweet scent. From her vantage point on the floor, she could see the spot where the drop of poison had fallen. The stone had fractured there, turning to fine dust around the base of the plant. She sat on the floor in her thin night dress, heedless of the chill.

Jancy found her there a while later.

"What's this?" She came to stand beside Amira with fresh candles in her hand.

Her presence broke the trance holding Amira. She peered up into the bright candlelight. "My brother?"

"He's too small. Too weak. They say he will not last the day."

"Help me dress. I must see him."

"Mistress, you shouldn't be wandering about in the castle. You're not well."

"Then bring him here." She had never been so sure of anything in her life. She had to help. Deep inside, she knew she could.

"I will help you dress, but I was sent for the jar."

"Leave the jar. Bring me instead."

"I'm sorry, I can't. I don't have anything in place to help you yet." Jancy grabbed the shimmering jar and then dashed for the door.

Not willing to miss her chance, Amira ran after her. Whether it was the long sleep or the excitement, she managed to reach the door before it closed. For the first time, she glimpsed the hallway. Two towering men in armor with swords at their sides stood four strides away. The guards gasped. The maid spun around, looking horrified.

"Mistress, please, you must go back inside."

The hallway stretched out in front of Amira. The space was so long and narrow it seemed to close in around her. The flames of the torches on the walls danced as though a breeze had just blown past them all. Amira turned around only to see a solid wall behind her. There was nowhere for a breeze to come from. When she turned back to the maid, she found the guards had their eyes squeezed shut.

"What are you doing?" How could they guard against anything if they couldn't see?

"Please, let's go back into your room." Jancy reached for Amira's arm.

"I have to see my brother."

"I'll be punished if you don't go back," whispered the maid. "Please. I'll do your father's bidding another time."

"My brother may die. I'll see that you're not punished. Take me to him. Now." She'd never talked to her maids with force before, but a life was at stake.

The torches flared. The guards stood very still, only their mouths moving.

Jancy shrank back a little as she nodded. "Yes, mistress."

The soft litany spoken by the guards reminded her of something Father used to do when she was younger, when he'd sit and watch her run around the room. The cadence of the words was familiar and comforting. It was a prayer, he'd said. For forgiveness. That had always seemed strange to her, but Father did strange things sometimes. Even Mother said so.

She'd never seen other men. Curiosity slowed her steps.

These men were tall and broad, like Father. Thick curly hairs covered their arms, and though they didn't have beards like he did, dark shadows colored their faces as though the hairs were just waiting to burst free.

"Why are your eyes closed?" she asked them.

Their prayer grew faster and louder.

"Mistress, please let them be. If you truly must, let's find your brother. Quickly." Jancy held out her hand.

Amira didn't take it, but she followed the maid. The winding hallway was dim, lit only by torches set at long intervals, offering just enough light to not fall into complete darkness between them. Her satin slippers did little to mask the roughness of the stone floor. The stones weren't even and neatly spaced like in her room.

In the distance, someone screamed. Something clanked and jangled loudly.

"What was that?" asked Amira.

"The other maids. The ones who angered the queen. Please don't make me become one of them," begged the maid.

Amira shivered, listening to the shuffling footsteps, moans, and chains dragging on stone. Sound traveled oddly through the castle. She wondered if the women were below them, deep in the belly of the castle somewhere. She felt bad for them. They'd done nothing wrong to be locked away. Maybe if she could help her brother, Mother would grant her a request. She could ask for the maids to be set free.

"If the king sent you, I'm sure he will protect you," Amira said confidently.

Jancy let out a long shuddering breath and nodded slowly. She started down the corridor again.

They made one more turn. Darkness stretched out ahead. The maid took the torch from the sconce and carried it with them. Amira hurried to keep up with the maid's longer strides.

"What is this place? Why are there no windows?" asked Amira. Father and the maids told her of wondrous things outside the castle, of the beautiful city of Katra.

Maybe it was night?

Jancy walked faster, keeping her gaze straight ahead.

Amira's skin prickled with goosebumps under her thin nightdress. "It's so cold."

"Would you like to go back to your room? We could find a beautiful dress for you to wear." The maid sounded so very hopeful.

If she went back, she might be warm, but the door would lock behind her and she'd never see her brother. "No."

"Very well." Jancy led them around a corner.

There were doors along both sides of this hall, doors with bars along the tops. She caught glimpses of hands wrapped around the bars, gaunt faces, and wide eyes that would shut quickly before she could look into them. A scream pierced the darkness again. Wailing followed. The maid moved quickly. Amira ran after her, not wanting to be left behind.

"Halt," called a man's voice from up ahead in the shadows.

"It's the princess," called the maid with a wavering voice. "She would see her brother."

"The queen will have our heads for this."

Amira and Jancy drew closer, turning another corner, to where they came to a lighted stairway and a guard posted at the bottom of it. A metal grated door stood between them and the stairway.

She glanced back into the darkness from which

they'd come, to the hallway lined with barred doors, and the twisted halls that ended with her room. The room where she'd spent all of her life.

"This is the dungeon?"

"Yes, mistress," whispered the maid, cowering near the guard who was staring into the darkness rather than looking at Amira.

Only Jancy would meet her eyes. Her maids always had, though they'd often avert them the first few days. She'd always assumed they were nervous or shy. There had been a lot of first days, so many in fact, that she'd long ago given up trying to learn their names. It was easier to not get too attached to them. Most were replaced without any warning from Mother. The maids seemed more at ease when she didn't talk to them very much anyway.

There was no ease in this maid now, or the guard for that matter. Both of them looked like they'd rather be on the other side of the grated door.

"Why is my room in the dungeon? Why will no one look at me?" she demanded of both of them.

Neither answered.

And why wasn't Father here to tell her what was happening if Mother was ill? Surely he would still talk to her at a time like this?

"Where is my father?"

The maid took a deep shuddering breath and let it out. "The king left for the country estate last night after your brother was born. That's where I'm from, but he did not say when he would return."

Maybe Father couldn't protect Jancy after all. If they were caught, Amira would have to try to talk Mother out of punishing Jancy. The maid had done nothing wrong.

"I'm sure you have questions." Jancy backed away further until her back hit the guard in the chest. "The Queen will no doubt answer them when she is feeling better."

"I'll see that you're not punished. If we move quickly, maybe she'll not even know I left my room."

Jancy turned to the guard and then back to Amira, shaking her head. "She'll know as soon as you ask her about the dungeon. Unless you can keep this all a secret?"

As hopeful as Jancy looked and as much as she wanted to keep the maid Father had sent safe, Amira didn't think she could manage to keep that secret. Not when she was the one at the heart of it. As if having her former maids sent to the dungeon wasn't bad enough, she was living there too? Anger boiled up inside her.

"Then take me to my brother. Now."

The torch beside Jancy and the guard flared. The two of them dodged aside as the flames roared.

"Yes, Mistress." Jancy tugged frantically at the guard and pointed him to the large lock on the door.

The guard hurried over and unlocked the door, swinging it into the room on silent hinges. The maid took the stairs two at a time. Amira followed, marveling at the smooth walls comprised of massive blocks of grey stone. Each step was a full slab of its own.

A large wooden door blocked their way at the top. Jancy unlocked it with a key she took from her skirt. "Please wait here a moment, Mistress. I will bring you a cloak so that you can move through the castle more easily."

Jancy could run off and bring Mother, or a host of guards to put her back in her room. But finding her brother without delay would also be helpful. "Leave me the key."

The maid nodded, placing the key in Amira's hand before she darted through the barely opened door. Looking over her shoulder to listen for the guard below, Amira waited. And waited.

Was the screaming and wailing still going on in the dungeon? What was being done to that poor person and who was doing it? Questions tumbled through her mind. The stairs remained silent and the wooden door absorbed any sound. The crack of light around the edges eventually tempted her to nudge it open just enough to peek through.

Something large and dark filled the brightness as the door suddenly opened farther. "Put this on," Jancy said.

Amira unfolded a dusky red cloak. She settled it around her shoulders, glad for the extra warmth. The weight was nothing compared to the dresses she normally wore. She pushed the door open enough to squeeze through.

"The hood. Quickly," urged the maid.

Amira tucked her long pale hair over her shoulder and dropped it into the hood, then pulled it over her head. She stepped into a wide hallway. Sunlight shown through a window, spilling warmth across the smooth stone floor. The brightness called to her, pulled at her. To see outside, at last, her heart ached for a glimpse of the sky she'd been told was blue.

THE PRINCE

"This way." Jancy tugged Amira away from the sunlight. She reached for Amira's hood, pulling it lower over her face.

"I can't see."

"And others can't see you. I'll guide you. If we hurry, we might get to your brother before the queen learns you're up here."

"Before you get in trouble, you mean."

"Yes." The maid pulled her along, slowing now and then as they traveled to avoid others.

So many voices, high-pitched and low, they all seemed to be talking at once and all around her. "Where are we?" Amira whispered.

"The great hall. We have to pass through here to get to the royal family's rooms. There will be more guards. Keep your head down and let me talk."

The voices had faded before the two of them were

stopped. A woman, metal clanking as she moved, called out, "Halt."

"We must see the Prince. I have brought a healer at the Queen's request," Jancy said.

"No one is to see the Prince. At the queen's request."

That couldn't be right. Mother would want to save her son, no matter what. She'd seen how sad Mother was when she'd lost the other babies.

"Please, you must let us pass. We have to hurry."

"The queen was clear. No one is to see the prince. None shall pass." A heavy thump from the butt of her spear accompanied her declaration. Armor creaked. "If you do not leave at once, I will have you sent to the dungeon."

"You will not." Amira pulled the hood from her face. "You will allow us to see the prince."

The guard shrieked and covered her eyes with one hand. The other held tight to her spear. "Trees take us all! We're doomed." The guard darted past them with hurried steps.

"Stop," Amira commanded. She'd never employed the tone of voice Mother so often used, but if she didn't now, the guard would bring others. Her brother might die.

The woman went still, both of her feet on the floor and her back to them.

"You will stay here at your post, and you will tell no one we are here."

The woman said nothing but also did not move.

That would have to do. Amira put her hood back in place and the maid led her onward.

Jancy's plea worked on the next guard but not on the thick dark-skinned man at the door to her brother's room.

"I cannot let you pass. The queen has ordered that no one is to enter," said the guard.

A baby cried inside. Amira closed her eyes, sinking into the darkness of the hood so she could focus on the pleas of her brother.

"He's scared," she said. "He needs me."

"Go back," said the guard. "I will not let you pass."

Jancy rested her hand on Amira's arm and sighed. "Mistress?"

The guards were all doing a fine job of following Mother's wishes, but they were also in Amira's way. Amira pulled back her hood once again.

"Sun and sky save us! Take him, if it means the rest of us can live."

The guard took two great strides before Amira said, "Stop."

He froze mid-step and fell to the floor mid-run, unmoving.

"What's happening to them?" whispered Amira.

"Hurry," Jancy beckoned her inside.

Amira pushed the door open. The shutters had been drawn, leaving the room in darkness. The prince's cries grew louder.

The brief glimpse of sunlight she'd seen earlier

made her hunger for more. "I need light. Open the window."

"Yes, mistress." The maid bumped into furniture on her way to the faint outline of the window.

Amira followed the frantic cries of her brother in the darkness. The shutter creaked as the maid worked to open it. Amira bumped into something waist-high. From the rough woven texture, she guessed it to be a basket. The cries were right next to her. She reached in.

Her fingers brushed over a tangle of cloth and a tiny warm hand. She held onto the little fingers, basking in the joy of finally meeting her brother. She'd waited her whole life for this. Even if she had to go back to her room in the dungeon, maybe Mother would bring him to visit. She grinned, thinking of all the things she could teach him and what they could play together. Her old toys were still in baskets, much like this one, under her bed. She hadn't looked at them in a long time. She hadn't felt well enough to play anything, and besides, she was getting too old for all of that.

It struck Amira then that she was long past due for her treatment. The poison might overwhelm her by the time Mother was feeling better. The thought of having to do the treatment on her own brought tears to her eyes. Even though Mother could be demanding and didn't tell her very much, not like Father did, she had very much missed her this morning.

If she could help her brother, that might help Mother feel better and then things could get back to how they should be.

Except, as she held her brother's hand he'd stopped crying, and she realized she didn't want to go back to her room. She wanted to stay here, with him. She didn't want to be alone anymore.

The shutter gave up its fight with a loud clatter. One side slammed against the wall while the other squeaked weakly when the maid pushed it aside. To Amira's dismay, the cloudy, bubble-filled glass allowed no cheery sunbeams into the room.

The dim light barely illuminated the room. A bed, stripped of all covers sat against one wall. One wooden stool sat beside it, tipped on its side, legs splayed in the air, much like the guard outside the door. Two chairs, both askew as if someone had sprung from them in a rush and no one had been back to put them to rights. Mother certainly would not have approved.

"I think he's happy that you're here," Jancy said from where she now stood by the door.

"Yes. He is." She could feel him, the flavor of his thoughts. He was different than Mother and Father, than all the maids. Everyone else was hollow inside, but her brother was warm and alive and overjoyed she was there with him.

Amira reached into the basket and picked up the wriggling bundle. The tangle of cloth caught on the edge of the basket. She pulled him free of the sour-smelling rags.

Jancy yelped. Amira turned to see her standing

with one hand on the door latch and the other over her mouth.

"What is it?"

Jancy pointed to the baby in her arms.

Amira looked down into the blackest eyes of her little brother and smiled. "No, nothing is wrong with you. You're perfect."

A dusting of fine white hair, just like hers, covered his little round head. His ears had the same point at the top of them as hers did. It was the thin tail that wrapped around her arm that made her giggle. The shimmering golden scales tickled as they slid over her skin. She held him closer to the light and realized the scaly patches covered much of his skin, including one cheek all the way up to his fuzzy white eyebrow.

"They're very pretty," she assured him. "Mother was foolish to say otherwise."

Amira looked to the maid. "Why would they leave him in that mess? Shouldn't a prince wear fine clothes?"

"He's a baby, mistress, one that likely won't last the night."

"Of course he won't. Not like this. How could she leave him starving and in rags?"

"Someday you'll understand, mistress. Best to leave him to the trees as an offering, but the queen wouldn't hear of it. She decreed the prince will pass in the castle."

With her brother in her arms, Amira walked to the window. Together, they would see Katra at last. She wrapped the edge of her cloak around his tiny pale form.

"He came too early, mistress. Best leave him now, nothing to be done for him."

The baby in her arms closed his eyes and stilled.

The sunlight she'd seen earlier called to her again, something about it tickled her mind. There wasn't enough here. She needed more. "Where is a window with more sun?"

"There's a private courtyard. The door is nearby."

They walked out of the room with the baby in Amira's arms. The guard was still on the floor, his eyes following the two of them, but his body didn't move.

"Why does he not get up?" she asked Jancy.

"He cannot. You..." she covered her mouth with a shaking hand.

The guard hadn't just been startled and lost his balance, she'd done something to him. Like the torches that had flared. Like her driving urge to feel the sunlight. Something had awakened and she felt stronger than she had in months.

But she'd hurt someone. Or at least it looked like she had. It couldn't be comfortable to fall like that or to stay there. "Get up," she said trying to remember the commanding tone of voice she'd used before. "You're free to return to your duty."

The guard scrambled to his feet and took off running.

"That may have been unwise, mistress." Jancy motioned for Amira to follow her. "We should go quickly if you wish to see the courtyard."

They hurried down another hallway and out the door at the end of it. The castle cast a shadow over half of the yard, but the other granted her a splendid view of the bright blue sky with puffs of white clouds dappling the perfection of it all. A bird landed on the branch of a tree beside Amira. It began to sing. She stepped into the sunlight and closed her eyes, drinking in the warmth. It lit her entire body, warming her very bones in a way that made her realize how cold she'd always been.

A gentle breeze rustled the leaves of the short trees and tugged at her hair, freeing it from the hood. As much as she wanted to enjoy this moment, to explore every inch of the courtyard and its treasures, her brother needed her. A fountain sat in the middle with a statue in its center. Water trickled from the top of a jar the stone woman held. Plants, some adorned with yellow flowers, floated atop the water. Half of the flat stones around the edge were in the light. She sat down and rested the baby on her lap. Green fuzzy moss filled the gaps between the stones underfoot. She kicked off her soiled slippers so that her toes could feel the soft fuzz. This place felt right, comfortable, like home, far more than her room ever had.

Her body seemed to know what it needed so she let instinct take over. Amira kept one hand on the baby and dipped the other into the chilly water of the little pond. Something nibbled at her fingers, but it didn't frighten her. Instead, it seemed to give her energy. More nibbles joined the first. The energy grew. The sunlight helped too, and even the moss under her feet. She thought of the lilies that had sprung from her floor. One drop of the poison in her veins had done that. But she'd also seen it hurt people. Unsure of how to use it right, she tried to find a different way to help her brother.

The energy gathered inside her until it became a burning that filled her chest. She pulled her hand from the water and balanced her toes on the stones where they didn't touch any moss. She waited a moment, but the burn didn't get any worse. Relieved, Amira tried to understand how to take this energy and do something helpful with it.

In her mind she imagined the baby on her lap was bigger, healthy, with rosy cheeks and bright eyes. This was the face she remembered when she thought of her friend long ago. Her brother would be a little boy who laughed, who was wise and smart like Father. He would be her friend, her playmate. Someone who would never leave without a word, or she amended, leave her like Father had.

She held his tiny hands in her own and leaned down to kiss him on the cheek.

The burning flowed through her, out her mouth, and onto his skin. It sizzled in the air all around them.

The door to the courtyard burst open. The queen rushed in and slammed it closed behind her. "No one comes in until I say so," she yelled. A fine sheen of sweat covered her face. Her hands trembled where she held onto the door she now leaned against.

The queen wore a plain shift under an embroidered

dressing gown that hung loosely around her shoulders. The jewels she'd worn earlier were gone as was the golden glow of her skin. Shadows had settled below her eyes. Her hair hung in a tumble, curls spilling over her face and back. She shoved them aside so that the fury on her face was impossible to miss.

"Amira, what have you done?"

5

A New Monster

Jancy cowered in the shadows. Amira stared at the queen in her disarray. She had seen Mother angry before, but that had been aimed at the maids, never at her.

"Mother, you are unwell. Please, sit."

The queen didn't move. "They said you took the baby. That you froze the guards." She shook her head. "You shouldn't be out here. Up here. Everyone is talking, rumors are across half of Katra by now. Oh Amira, you've ruined everything."

Tears rolled down Mother's cheeks. "Your father has left me, my son is dying, and your health is fading fast. Katra will fall into chaos again."

"My brother isn't dying."

She knew that now with a certainty deep in her heart. His feet kicking against her stomach assured her that her heart was telling the truth. She let go of his hands. He started to cry.

"Shh, no one is leaving you alone again. I promise." She picked up the now chubby baby. Thick dark hair brushed against her chin. Her heart skipped a beat. He looked nothing like her now. His skin was a ruddy tan like Mother and Father, his hair dark like theirs, and his eyes too. Even his tail had vanished. He squirmed in her lap, flailing his fat little fingers until he grabbed a handful of her long white hair. He cooed happily.

It wasn't until he turned toward Mother, who was creeping closer, that Amira spotted a patch of tiny golden scales on the boy's cheek. Right where she'd kissed him. They shimmered in the sunlight.

"He's not a monster anymore," Mother whispered. She knelt on the ground just out of reach and held out her arms. "Please, give him to me."

"I think he would like that very much. Unless...you don't mean to leave him in that room again, do you? Or put him in the dungeon? You'll be good to him?"

Tears glittered in Mother's eyes. She nodded.

Amira placed the prince in Mother's arms, untangling her hair from his fingers as she did so. Once he was safely settled, she sat back down in the sun. She felt weak and tired, but not like after her treatments, more like she remembered feeling after running around her room all morning. It was a good kind of tired.

"I think I'm hungry," she announced to no one in particular. Her stomach twisted as she tried to think about what sounded good. Nothing. Then she remembered the energy that had flowed through her from the water and the moss.

Amira turned around and parted the floating plants. Below the surface, once the water cleared, swam a school of bright orange fish. She reached down, plunging her fingers into the cool water, and stroked the soft frilly fin of one of them. The fish crowded closer, their heads bobbing out of the water. She giggled.

"Mistress?" Jancy crept from the shadows. "Would you like me to send for something to eat?"

"No. I'm starting to feel better now. Thank you." She lifted her head to the sun, basking in the warmth and light. A flock of birds descended into the courtyard, filling the nearby tree with song. One of them flew closer. First landing on the ground by the hem of her cloak, then hopping closer. It fluttered up onto her lap and then her shoulder, where it nuzzled against her cheek. The soft feathers slid against her skin like the fine silk of her dresses. She stroked the feathers on the top of its head and down between its wings. It twittered happily and then flew off to rejoin the others in the tree.

Amira's heart swelled. She'd never felt this happy, not even when she was rolling on the floor with laughter with her friend or snuggling next to Father while he read her a story. It was as though her entire body wanted to giggle but that wasn't enough. She jumped to her feet and ran around the courtyard.

Mother didn't scold her. She was too busy rocking the baby and running her hands over his bare skin.

Amira's fingers danced over the waxy leaves of

the plants, the smooth petals of flowers, and the rough bark of the trees. Everything was alive and invigorating. She spun in circles with her arms outstretched. Her feet tangled in the spinning cloak and she tumbled to the ground, still laughing.

"We should go inside," Mother said at last. "I must send a message to the king."

She tried to stand with the baby in her arms but her feet got caught in her dressing gown. Amira took the baby from her and Jancy helped Mother to her feet.

"We will go first. Wait here a moment, Amira." Mother went inside with Jancy.

Amira held her brother who now looked nothing like her and studied him closely. He seemed well enough, healthy and strong. The scaled patch on his cheek was rough, much like the bark of the tree. She hoped it would fade in time, that he'd look just like Father so that Mother would love him.

When Mother opened the door and beckoned her inside, Amira paused. Could she go back to her bedroom where the sun didn't warm her skin? She didn't want to hurt anyone, but she also didn't want to return to that room. And she didn't want to be tired anymore.

"I'll stay out here."

"Don't be foolish, Amira. Come inside."

She shook her head.

"Please come in and get dressed. You must be chilled through."

"I'm warmer than I've ever been."

Mother opened the door wider, beckoning with open arms. "Amira, give me the baby."

"I don't want any more treatments," Amira said.

"But we need your blood. I'll explain everything, just come inside."

A pit formed in Amira's stomach, weakening her knees, making her entire body shake. "My blood? You mean, the poison?"

Mother smiled weakly.

"Was there a curse?" Amira asked, desperate for an answer that would cut short her spiraling thoughts.

Mother's head shook the slightest bit, certainly not the nod Amira had hoped for.

All of the years of treatments. All the bottles that had been filled with shimmering gold. Her blood. And Mother had known the truth all along.

Mother licked her lips, her gaze darting around the courtyard and up to the sky. "Amira, please. I'll explain. Don't be angry. Just come inside."

The prince started to cry. Clouds swelled overhead and turned grey. "No. I want Father."

"He's not here." Mother stared at the darkening sky. "Please."

Amira looked once more at the baby in her arms. The excitement of meeting her brother had vanished. The truth was clear to see. "He's *not* my brother."

"Not exactly, no." Mother held out her hands.

She looked Mother straight in the eyes. The truth twisting around her gut was as clear as the fear she saw there. "I am not your daughter."

"Of course not." Her lips drew into a sneer. "You're Spindelkin. At least you're not one of the feral forest vermin like the rest. You can thank us for that."

The floor seemed to drop out from under Amira. A chill came over her. Thunder rolled in the distance.

"Give me the baby," demanded the queen.

"You left him to die." Amira spotted Jancy behind her mother and remembered what she'd said. "You wouldn't even give him to the trees like anyone else would have. Maybe I will give him to the trees for you."

The queen gasped. "No."

The prince cried louder, his hands and feet flailing.

Amira tried to calm him, to speak to him, but he was no longer like her. He was hollow inside like everyone else.

"You know nothing of the Spindelkin," said the queen. "If you take my son, I shall set fire to the Spindelskov. The never-ending forest will be nothing more than a vast field of ash."

The flock of birds in the tree began to squawk, filling the courtyard with a wild racket.

"You said you would explain," said Amira.

The queen spun around. "You'll have your explanation when my son is back in my arms and you are in your room."

"In the dungeon."

The queen held her chin high and scowled at Amira. "Yes, in your room filled with beautiful things, wearing the finest of gowns, and eating the same food that I eat. You are treated like a princess. That was the deal that was made and I have abided by it for eleven years. In return, Katra flourishes."

"But I am not flourishing," said Amira.

"No." A flicker of the warm woman who had sat beside her during her treatments when she was far younger, who had comforted her, passed over the queen's face. "You are not."

She'd never considered that Mother hadn't loved her. Not until today. Not until she'd seen how the queen looked at her real son now that he was like her. Not until there was talk of an agreement, how it wasn't poison in her veins, how Mother had lied. For eleven years.

Tears welled in Amira's eyes and her throat grew thick. She backed further into the courtyard.

The birds took flight, fluttering around Amira.

"What did you do with my blood?"

"Your blood helped Katra. Every drop went to something good, benefitted someone. Nothing was ever wasted."

She couldn't believe what she was hearing. "Good? You told me I was cursed. You told me that you were helping me. But you were draining me, every day, taking more. You saw how weak I was. You would have killed me?"

"It was necessary. You wouldn't understand," the queen said quietly.

The queen was right. Amira couldn't understand.

Everything she'd known was untrue. Her home, her parents, her own body. They'd told her she was different because of the curse, but the prince had been like her. Mother had called him a monster. Was she a monster too?

Amira wiped at the tears running down her cheeks.

Tiny black creatures raced across the rocks, their multitude of legs creating a blur she couldn't track. They rushed up her cloak and raced over the baby, extruding white silk as they traveled.

She'd seen a fair number of spiders in her bedroom, but never this many at once, never moving this fast or making webs on her, over her, binding the baby to her arms and chest. How was she supposed to do anything with her arms pinned to the baby?

One of the birds again landed on her shoulder. It chirped softly in her ear. The others quieted but flew around her, weaving their own wall between her and the queen.

The bird chirped again, this time she made out a word. "Home."

"What?" She turned to the bird.

Its beady black eye blinked once. "Fly home."

Maybe the bird wasn't very smart. "I don't have wings."

"We fly."

The spiders finished their work, covering her torso all the way around with a thick web. They skittered down her cloak, a rush of black over the red fabric, and then vanished into the cracks and shadows of the courtyard as quickly as they'd assembled.

"Don't take him from me," begged the queen.

Amira couldn't hand him over if she wanted to. In fact, she was having a hard time staying on her own feet with the heavy weight of the baby on her chest and her arms pinned down. Wings buffeted her from all sides, sending her hair flying. One by one, the birds sunk their tiny talons into her cloak until they covered her back and shoulders.

She looked down at the perfect child and then to the woman who had left him to die. "I'm sure my own mother said the same thing."

"She didn't. Your kind doesn't know anything about love."

Amira thought she did, but everything she'd loved had been a lie. "Goodbye...Mother."

Her feet left the ground, toes dragging until they too lifted into the air. With a great chirping commotion, the birds flapped and fluttered until her feet cleared the top of the tree where they had rested. She bobbed up and down as their wings beat, lifting her higher and higher.

For better or worse, Amira was going home.

6

Companions

The dark clouds that had gathered began to drift away. The queen yelled and ran after Amira, arms lifted high, but the birds had found their rhythm now. When they finally cleared the walls of the courtyard, Amira could see all around her.

Four towers marked the corners of the castle. Guards walked the parapet that joined them. They looked up, waving their arms. One reached for a bow. Then he must have caught sight of who it was and quickly turned away. The screams of the queen faded as the birds flew Amira toward the stables. Horses were so much bigger than Amira had imagined. Even from up in the sky, they were larger than the people nearby. Women and children in brown clothes like Jancy had worn, knelt in the long rows of plants along one side of the castle. They tossed colorful objects into baskets. Stone roads ran from the castle into the sprawl of buildings around it. Horses pulled carts through the streets. Men and women held their hands up to their eyes and gazed in wonder as she flew overhead. Children pointed and called out. She must have been too high now for them to see who she was. Or what she was, as none of them looked away.

Tidy squares of buildings sat together, lined by roads. They became narrower further from the castle and then turned to rutted dirt. Fields covered hillsides. Men and women toiled there as well, using great horned cows to pull plows through the soil. Others gathered rocks. Some were assembling a low stone wall. Over the next hill stood a flock of shaggy sheep, their black faces almost lost in the long white wool. A man on a horse sped from the castle and down the road in the same direction the birds were taking her. Dust billowed behind him as the horse galloped along. He seemed to be having no problem holding on. She couldn't imagine riding such a beast. Its mane blew in the rider's face as he bent low over its neck.

She wondered where they were going. Maybe to the King? She'd never know. The rider faded into the distance as the birds carried her away.

After a while, the birds started to fly lower, their wings losing their steady beat. They glided downward until Amira's feet came to rest in a field of wildflowers. Tall trees lined the meadow.

"More come," said the bird near her ear.

The flock who had taken her this far flew off to land in one of the nearby trees. One by one, giant black birds lifted from other trees and flew toward her. This new flock sunk their talons into her cloak and lifted her upward.

Amira might have wished she were more the size of her maids or the king and queen, but she supposed the birds were grateful she was small. The baby weighed heavy on her chest. Thankfully he was sound asleep because a wailing infant flying through the air would surely draw more attention than their silent flight.

The city she had so longed to see, had imagined in dreams all her life, disappeared behind her. Here and there, cottages popped up in the hills and woods. Animals of all sorts stood nearby, creatures she tried to put names to from the stories Father used to tell. A child spotted her far above and ran, pointing upwards and shouting. He plowed through a flock of chickens, scattering them in all directions.

The baby woke but did not cry. He sucked on his fingers, creating a warm wet spot that seeped into her nightdress. When the sun began to sink on the horizon, the black birds set her down near a stand of white-barked trees. Amira fell onto her backside and sat, trying to work her hands free of the webbing. A small brown furry creature with black and white stripes on his back darted over. It stood still for a moment, watching her and then seeming to decide she meant it no harm, scurried onto her cloak where it began to chew through the web. Once the creature had a tear started, she wiggled her hand loose and helped. At last, the web fell free. Amira grabbed the baby just before he fell backward onto her lap.

She wriggled her other hand past the leaves and into the loose soil beneath them. Amira pushed the energy she took from the ground into the baby until he slept once more. Then she took a little for herself. A giant furry creature loped out of the trees and came to sit nearby. It glanced over its shoulder at her, golden eyes meeting her own. It yipped softly, "Safe."

Amira nodded and closed her eyes.

When she opened them again, the sky was still dark. Her guardian met her gaze and then slipped back into the trees. Amira got up and stretched. Energy hummed through her body. She'd never felt so alive. The trees and plants each had their own feel, their own flavor. She could sense that they were overjoyed to have her among them. She walked a small circle, keeping the baby in sight as she took a moment to touch each tree and bush she passed. It was as though they sighed wistfully when she did so, their colors suddenly more vibrant and new leaves and growth unfurling.

Another creature, this one larger than her nighttime guardian but smaller than a horse, stepped shyly from the trees. Great horns erupted from its head, spreading left and right like white branches. Large brown eyes blinked at her.

"Ride?" it asked

Amira eyed its rounded back. She supposed she could ride it like the man had ridden the speeding horse. She nodded and went to gather up the baby.

The creature knelt in the leaves, making it easy for her to step over it with the baby in her arms. She settled onto the boney back. When it stood, her feet left the ground, but the ground wasn't that far away.

As the creature wove its way back into the trees, she wondered why Father's stories had never mentioned this. There had been stories of Katra, princesses, mischievous children, blacksmiths, farmers, millers, and shopkeepers, but no one had ever flown with the birds or ridden wild creatures. His stories never mentioned forests at all. The only time she'd seen the Spindelskov was on the maps he brought now and then. He didn't speak of it much other than to say that those that dwelt in the trees had no use for the folk of Katra. From the fear she'd witnessed in the castle, it seemed the people of Katra had no desire to deal with the Spindelkin either.

The beast leapt lightly over fallen logs and dodged trees with ease. Its antlers brushed against leaves as it ran. Amira concentrated on holding the baby and not falling off. Every time he woke, she pushed him back to sleep in his mind. She regretted not taking Jancy with her to tend to the baby, but they would not have been able to travel as fast or by these means. Amira hoped Jancy would be able to escape the castle on her own so the queen couldn't send her to the dungeon.

Would the queen send soldiers after her? She tried to remember the maps her father had shown her. Soldiers would likely take roads. They would be far behind by now. Amira sent a burst of gratitude to the beast. She didn't know what she would have done without the help of the creatures.

When they finally slowed, the sun was high overhead. The beast had brought them to the side of a creek. It knelt once again, offering her an easy dismount. Her legs and back were sore and the clear water looked quite inviting. She approached the creekside, picking her way over the flat rocks. The beast hung its mighty head low and drank. Seeing that it was safe, Amira knelt and scooped up a handful of water, drinking it down in one gulp. The cool sweet water quenched a thirst she hadn't realized she'd had. It was so much better than the water she'd drank all her life. Wild, free water, untainted by buckets and wells. With each sip she took, she felt a little more alive.

"Better"? asked the beast.

She nodded.

"Elk," it said, bobbing its head up and down.

Father had mentioned elk before. Hunters killed them for food. She may have even eaten the meat. She rarely asked what had been on her plate. None of it was satisfying, not exactly distasteful, but never what she hungered for. Food made her stomach stop grumbling, but it didn't make her grow, not like everyone else. She saw that the baby was awake and fed him more energy. Was it her imagination or was he getting bigger each time she fed him?

Amira pulled him fully onto her lap. He did sit higher against her chest, his head taller, face rounder.

He cooed happily. It occurred to her that he hadn't made any waste since she'd first held him. Maids had often chattered about their children, how infants needed frequent changing. But that wasn't the case at all. For that matter, she hadn't felt the need either. It seemed energy worked differently than regular food and water. She had so much to learn. She hoped the Spindelkin would be willing to teach her. And that they would let her stay.

When she glanced up, the elk was gone. She got to her feet with the baby in her arms. What was she going to do now? She didn't know where to go.

A tiny mouse skittered over her bare foot. "Follow," it squeaked. Amira tried, but it was difficult as there was no clear path and the mouse easily vanished under leaves and underbrush.

"I can't see you," she said. It was odd talking to a mouse, knowing it could talk back if it chose to. The mice she'd spotted in her room had never spoken to her. Or maybe they had but she'd been too weak to understand them.

The mouse peeked out from under a tuft of tall grass. Its little head hung low.

"What's the matter?" She reached down and scooped up the mouse. It didn't try to run away. Instead, it fluffed itself up and snuggled against her fingers.

"If I hold you, can you show me which way to go?"

The mouse nodded, looking much happier.

"Good. Let's be off then."

She held the baby with one hand and the mouse with the other, but that got tiring very quickly now that the baby was so much heavier. The mouse skittered up her arm and onto her shoulder where it chittered if she went the wrong way.

They traveled until the sun disappeared through the leaves and the forest grew dark. Amira sat down, her legs and back grateful for a break. The mouse nuzzled against her cheek and then scampered off.

Like the night before, golden eyes shown in the dim light of the forest. "Wolf," it said. "Sleep."

Amira curled up with the baby against her chest and closed her eyes. Her body was too tired to ask any questions of the wolf.

The next day she was led by a bear and then a badger. At night an owl kept watch over her. For the next three days, she fed herself and the baby from the soil and plants around her as they traveled through grassy hills, taking turns on the backs of a small herd of elk.

When it was nearly nightfall, they came to a stop on the top of a high hill. In the distance lay a stretch of forest as far as she could see. Towering trees ran up over mountains to one side and to the shore of a vast ocean on the other, spilling down the middle into the darkness of twilight. She'd reached the Spindelskov at last.

7

Home

Amira started to bed down with the Elk in the tall grass as she had the past few nights, but one of them nudged her toward the trees.

"It will be dark before we get there. I don't know what to do."

"Go," it said.

She wished the animals had more to say. Though they were helpful, speaking with words did not seem to come naturally to them. Gathering up the baby in her cloak, she cautiously made her way through the grass. The downward slope made for easy travel, but she had to be careful not to gain too much forward speed with the baby or she would fall down the hill.

The moon had risen and floated overhead before Amira came to the first of the tall trees. To call them tall was laughable. The forests she'd traveled through to get here were full of tall trees. The narrow trees in the distance seemed to shoot straight to the sky. The trees directly before her were covered in green needles from a point far above to the branches that hung just over her head. They offered a ceiling of sorts, blocking light from above and keeping the underbrush to a minimum while allowing plenty of space to move about. It was certainly much easier to make her way into the Spindelskov than it was to navigate the other forests she'd been in.

She knew the baby was awake by the fact that he was moving around, but she couldn't see him very well. In fact, she couldn't see much of anything at all. The way ahead was pitch black. Unsure what to do next, and tired from her walk down the steep hill, Amira sat, only to discover that the fallen needles poked through her cloak. The birds had made numerous holes when they'd carried her and her nightdress was very thin. The air grew cold. Low fog slipped over her like a chilly sheet. She clutched the baby closer. He squirmed and started to cry.

From the blackness, a soft glow crept toward her. A woman, not much taller than Amira, walked through the trees as if she'd memorized their positions long ago. She wore a shining silver dress with a high collar that came almost to the top of her head, fanning out into a circle toward her shoulders. White jewels glimmered at the edge of the collar, down her sleeves, and around the hem of her dress. Light seemed to emanate from her skin, making her glow. Long white hair like Amira's flowed down to her waist.

It was her face that made Amira's mouth go

dry. A face she'd felt but never seen. A high, thin nose, impossibly large eyes, and a narrow mouth. Long, thin fingers, like her own, reached out to Amira.

Her voice held a lilting accent, soft and almost musical. "We were told of your coming. We have been waiting for you."

The woman cocked her head and her brow creased. "You have brought a human into our world. The elders will need to decide what to do with it."

"He is a prince of Katra."

The woman's eyes opened even wider, her white brows rose high on her smooth forehead. "Does this prince have a name? We were told no royal children had survived. They are sickly poor people, those that dwell in the city."

Amira's mind raced. The people of Katra did not name their children for a full year, but Amira couldn't call him baby for all that time. She thought of a story her father used to tell, one of children who lived in Katra. The prince deserved to have a name that belonged to his own people.

"Corvin. Prince Corvin. He was born only six days ago. News may not have reached you yet."

The woman smiled knowingly. "We heard of a boy child born too early, one who would not survive any longer than his siblings. I told you the people of Katra are weak."

"I fixed him. He is healthy now."

"And much older than he should be." The woman

fixed her in an accusing stare. "The elders will wish to speak to you as well. You are not as much of a child as you appear."

Was she in trouble? Amira clutched Corvin to her chest. "I'm Amira."

The woman bowed from her waist. "Cordella. It's getting late, we will sort this out in the morning. Does the child require food?"

"I have been feeding him from the ground and trees. It makes him grow though. Soon he'll be walking on his own." She laughed nervously.

Cordella frowned. "As I said, the elders will sort this out. You have broken the rules of the Spindelkin."

Amira's feet seemed as rooted as the trees. "I didn't know the rules."

"All Spindelkin know the rules, Amira. You can plead your case to the elders. Perhaps they will be merciful."

Cordella took Amira's shoulder and guided her deeper into the trees. Her glow offered the forest an otherworldly light, magical, and a bit scary. She was glad for Cordella's hand on her shoulder, assuring her she wasn't alone. And that she was with her kind at last. Even if she'd broken rules.

The needled trees gave way to thinner trunks but with leaves far atop them. Moonlight shown down through the branches, easing her fears. She missed the animals, the ones who had guided her here. The Spindelskov seemed too quiet. Even their footsteps were swallowed by the fallen leaves and needles. The silence was only broken by Corvin sucking on his fingers and the occasional swish of Amira's cloak or Cordella's skirts.

"Are we alone?" Amira finally asked.

"This close to the border, mostly, yes. Sentries are placed along the border, but they're up high, you wouldn't see them from the ground."

"They climb these trees?"

"Oh yes. You have not climbed a tree?"

"I've never seen trees until six days ago."

Cordella's brows rose again. "You'll be climbing one soon enough, though with stairs. Can't very well climb a tree properly in a dress, can we?"

Amira hazarded a smile.

When Cordella smiled back, Amira felt more at ease. But the talk of breaking rules and pleading for mercy made her stomach knot. As long as they let her stay outside and didn't lock her away like the queen had, she would take what punishment they saw fit.

They walked onward for a short while before coming to a stop. Amira looked around. It was hard to make out her surroundings beyond Cordella's glow, like a shuttered candle.

"You'll be safe with us tonight in Gorsia, little one." Cordella held out her hand. She led Amira to a spiraling staircase that surrounded one of the tree trunks.

If Cordella hadn't stopped her there, Amira would have walked right past it. The stairs blended in perfectly with the trunk, even having bark of their own. She looked up at the tree. Stairs went up as far as she could see.

Whatever lay above them was invisible from the ground.

"Go ahead, I'll be right behind you."

Amira took a tentative step. The stair wasn't hard like the stone stairs that had taken her out of the dungeon. The surface was smooth and warm, almost like it was living. They seemed to eat up the sound of her footsteps. Their size and height made them comfortable to climb. They made her feel like she was the size she was meant to be rather than far too small.

She climbed, round and round. When she looked down, she spotted Cordella following a ways behind, her soft glow making her easy to spot in the moonlight. Almost as though she was a moon herself.

After a while, Amira noticed sounds, and voices near and far. She slowed and studied the surrounding trees. People were moving on them, around them, on platforms, and in buildings. Buildings up in the trees. She laughed to herself.

Amira came to a stop as the stairs leveled onto a platform. More rose higher but she stepped off to wait for Cordella. Bridges ran from this platform to others on trees across the way. Like roads up in the sky, they spanned the trees. All of the Spindelkin emitted a soft glow. She checked her skin and found it pale but not luminescent like the others.

When Cordella arrived, Amira asked, "Why don't I glow like you?"

"That is a very good question. One I hope the elders will be able to answer. You look like one of us, but yet, you don't. Something is not quite right."

"The queen said I was cursed as a baby."

Cordella waved her hand. "Katra's Queen is full of lies." She pointed to one of the bridges. "Take that one. You'll find an empty dwelling at the end of it. You may use that for tonight. I'll be by to get you in the morning."

"Thank you."

Amira held Corvin tightly as they traveled over the bridge. She tried very hard not to look over the vine-covered railing. Only blackness lay below. They were far too high to see any hint of the ground. The leaves did a fine job of masking them. She certainly hadn't seen any hint of this tree city from the ground, even with the Spindelkin glowing as they did.

Corvin grabbed hold of her hair and tugged hard. She twisted her head to one side to keep it from tearing out, but that put her off balance. Her hip hit the railing. The whole bridge rocked from side to side. Amira grabbed the railing with one hand. With her eyes closed, she inched her way toward the end of the bridge. One foot in front of the other, her hand pulling her along while her heart pounded in her chest.

When her foot hit a solid surface, one that didn't rock and sway, she cracked one eye open to find she'd reached the platform.

A wooden structure, like one of the tiny huts she'd seen in the hills beyond Katra, grew around the trunk of the tree, part of it. The trunk shot upwards, lost in the next layer of leaves. A cloth hung over the doorway. She pulled it aside and went in. It was dark there without her own glow to light the room. But the moon shown in enough when she held the cloth open to see what must have been a bed of sorts on the floor. She'd only ever slept in her big bed in the castle or on the ground with the animals during her travels. The mattress appeared to be made of heavy cloth stuffed full of something that crunched when she sat on it. But it was better than the wooden floor or the ground. She settled in with Corvin snuggled against her. Amira gave him a bit of energy one last time for the day. His breathing grew light and steady moments later. Amira drifted off to sleep, wondering what her meeting with the elders would hold.

SUNLIGHT

Cordella pulled the cloth door aside, letting in the morning light that filtered down through the leaves. "Good morning. Did you sleep well?"

Corvin had, but Amira had been restless. In all her dreams, faceless elders banished her from the Spindelskov. They sent her back to Katra to be locked away in the dungeon where it was cold and she never saw the sun again.

"Will we meet with the elders now?" Amira asked.

"After we greet the sun. You are familiar with that custom, surely?"

Amira shook her head. "Will you show me?"

"Come on then. Try to follow along. Can you leave the baby here?"

Visions of Corvin rolling out of the bed and over the edge of the platform filled her with worry. "I don't think that would be wise."

Cordella sighed. "Bring him then. Hurry, we don't want to be late."

They walked out of the hut and back over the bridge to climb the stairs. They went round and round, higher and higher. Other Spindelkin joined them on the upward trek. The higher they went, the more she could feel the tree sway. The breeze hadn't been noticeable when they'd begun this ascent. Now it toyed with her hair, batting the strands over her eyes.

Corvin whined, his little fingers digging into her skin as if he could sense her trepidation.

"We'll be fine," she assured him and herself.

The platforms toward the top were narrower, but more plentiful, scattered along the main branches of the trees up where the sun was much brighter. Spindelkin gathered in clumps upon the platforms, their hands joined with those around them, faces raised to the sun.

Cordella's hand slipped into Amira's. A man came to stand on her left side. He reached out but saw she was holding Corvin. He scowled and went to stand beside Cordella instead. Amira did her best to stand still like the others and ignore the swaying of the tree and the wind blowing her hair into her face.

The warm sun shown down. She closed her eyes against the light that blinded her in flashes as the leaves fluttered. Like in the courtyard in Katra, a soft flow of energy began to fill her. Cordella tugged Amira's fingers.

Amira peeked to see what she was doing. The others were all rolling their heads from left to right in slow circles. A hum rose, like one of the insects that had pestered her when she'd slept outside on her journey to Spindelskov. The sound filled the air, reverberating through the platform under her feet. An awareness of all that was around her seeped into her mind. Everyone around her, the men, women, and children, they were all part of her and she of them. Her heart swelled. These were her people. Her family.

Cordella squeezed Amira's hand. But this time it wasn't because she'd missed something. A feeling of rightness flowed from Cordella into Amira. She did belong here, They were one, connected, all of the Spindelkin. Tears spilled down her cheeks.

Corvin began to cry.

The humming broke from its one note into a discordant fumble. Faces turned from the sun to stare at her. From everywhere. Spindelkin filled the trees around them, as far as she could see.

"Go down. Now. Hurry," Cordella whispered.

Amira dashed for the stairs and hurried downward, heedless of the swaying and the shuffle of footsteps above. Cordella followed close behind.

"That baby will ruin you. And you're ruining him. Changing him. Don't you see it?"

Amira shook her head. "I don't understand."

"You're feeding him from yourself. In our way. But he's not Spindelkin. The more you feed him, the more connected to you he will be. He must be returned to his kind and be nourished in the way of his people."

Amira had an idea. "Take me to the elders."

9

JUDGEMENT

It was midday before Cordella had convinced the elders to hear Amira rather than banish her from the Spindelskov for interrupting the morning ritual.

She sat before the six men and women on the ground beneath the trees. A scattering of green ferns surrounded them, poking from great moss-covered boulders. A long silence stretched out.

Amira looked everywhere but at the six figures in front of her. In the dappled green light, she made out a towering rock face to her right. Trees grew from it at precarious angles, reaching upward, their roots spilling over the rock edge like fingers. Water burbled off to her left. Something rustled in the fallen leaves behind her. The air smelled of wet soil.

"You are the child," a voice like a creaking tree said at last.

"Who should not be a child," said another.

Amira peeked at the elders. The six of them had skin like the bark of trees, rough and wrinkled, their hair long and white. They wore their hair in braids that pooled around them where they sat. White stones adorned the strands like tiny stars, sparkling in the sunlight that filtered down through the trees. Their robes were the soft green of a newborn leaf. The more she allowed herself to focus on them, she could see the edges of leaves.

They wore clothes made from leaves themselves. Yet the leaves weren't hard or discolored like those that fell to the ground. They were still living. Their clothes were alive.

"I don't understand," she said.

"Time moves differently here," said one of the men. His beard hung down to his lap. Twigs and glossy stones adorned the lengthy tumble.

"You've been far from the trees," said one of the others.

"Starved," said another.

The voices built upon each other.

"Kept a child."

"So strange."

"No longer one of us," said a woman so old that her skin appeared to have moss growing in the deepest crevices.

"Broke the rules."

One scrambled closer, moving through the underbrush in silence. Had she not been looking directly at it approaching, the elder would have seemed to have been in one place one breath and right in front of her the next. As it was, when a pale hand reached out and grabbed Corvin from her lap, she barely found the air to gasp.

"Give him back!" She tried to get to her feet, but another of the elders held her down. For as old and fragile as they appeared to be, they were strong and quick. "Please, don't hurt him."

"You have marked this one," announced the woman holding Corvin. She stroked the golden scales on his cheek.

"I didn't mean to. I only tried to save him. I don't know how it happened."

One of the bearded men was suddenly before her. His stale breath buffeted against her face. "You have broken the rules."

"Cast her out," said the angry woman. "Out!"

"I don't even know the rules," said Amira.

The man pinched her shoulder. "All Spindelkin know the rules. We are born with the knowing."

"Then I have forgotten what I once knew. Please." She squirmed under the pressure he put on her shoulder. Corvin cried, his wails echoing off the rock face. The other elders crowded around her, their bodies blocking out the sun. Gnarled fingers pointed at her. Their voices joined in a rustle that hid their words.

The man behind her grabbed her other shoulder, holding her firmly to the ground while another pressed his forehead to her own. Like up on the tree tops, she got the sensation that he was sharing her mind, tasting her thoughts.

"You are Amira."

She nodded, her throat too tight to make words. Corvin's cries and the whispers of the other elders faded until there was only the man before her. His voice reverberated in her ears, vibrating through her body. The light, the trees, even the elder behind her, became a blur. Only the elder in front of her was clear.

"How do you know so little of your own people?"

"I don't remember ever being here before, but you look like me. You feel like me," she said.

"There are no Spindelkin outside the trees. We cannot live long without them."

"The queen said she made a deal with you, that there was a truce as long as I remained with her. I have been sick all my life, kept underground. It was only days ago that I saw the sun for the first time. The day I helped Corvin."

The elder pulled back a few inches to stare into her eyes, his own impossibly large and black. His lips puckered and then he sucked them in. They vanished beneath his beard. He chewed on them for a minute before they appeared again.

"We have no truce. There was no deal."

"But..."

He pondered her again, stroking his beard with long thin fingers. "You are Cantazia's child, I think." He touched her hair and then ran one finger down her cheek.

"You've been missing a long time. Stolen from us."

"The queen said she..."

He shook his head. "Lies. You were stolen. She will pay."

If that was true, if it had all been lies, then did she want the queen to pay? Perhaps. But not her father. Not the king, she corrected herself. He'd been kind. He'd been angry with the queen, angry enough to leave and live elsewhere.

"I have stolen her son. Isn't that enough?"

The elder grimaced. "We will send him back."

Sending Corvin back to Katra, to his parents seemed like a good thing. He had done nothing wrong. He deserved to know his mother and father, something the queen had taken from her. But part of her wanted him to stay. She'd grown attached to having him there, of his round, rosy-cheeked smile when she fed him. But he didn't belong here. The other Spindelkin didn't like him.

"Could he stay for just a little while longer?"

The elder shook his head. "That is not wise. He's been here too long already. Time moves differently in the trees, little one. You will see soon enough."

"I don't know what you mean."

"The child needs to eat in the way of his kind before it is too late. He will not survive here."

But the baby was plump, and his skin the color of his parents, eyes bright. He was the very image of health. "How could he not? It's beautiful here."

"To us, yes. But his kind doesn't belong here. He would see the truth of us soon enough. I would not see your heart broken, little one. We must send him back."

"But the queen said she would burn Spindelskov. Corvin is our protection."

The elder smiled kindly and patted her head. "The trees protect us. Katra's Queen can't hurt us here."

Sounds crept back in and time seemed to speed back up to normal. Corvin's cries hit her. She slipped out from under the hold of the elder behind her before time had fully righted itself.

Amira grabbed the baby from the elder woman. He quieted and sucked on his fingers.

"How would we send him back? If I take him, the queen will surely try to keep me there."

"You brought him," said the angry elder woman.

"The creatures brought them both," said the elder man who had spoken to her. "They will bring him back."

"Alone?" she asked. "He will need to eat. It took us days to get here. He'll be scared."

"You will feed him and then put him to sleep. We will see that he sleeps until he is home. His kind can care for him there."

"When?" she asked.

"Feed him now. You were at the sun ceremony this morning. You should be able. Give him all that you can and then send him to sleep.

She sat down, drawing energy from the ferns around her, listening to the water drip down the rock wall and up from the ground. The soft breathing of the elders around her. The leaves blowing high above. All of that she drew into herself and pushed into Corvin. When his bright eyes drifted closed, she brushed her lips over his cheek where she had kissed him before. "Sleep well little one."

His body expanded as she held him, growing heavier, his hair and limbs longer. When she finally tore her gaze from Corvin who was no longer a baby, she saw the six elders staring at her.

"Have I done something wrong again?"

"Not exactly," said the kind elder. "You need to stay here with us. You have much to learn. You have been too long from your people."

The elders beckoned to Cordella.

"Take Amira to a dwelling of her own. She will come to me after the sun each morning and then you will show her our ways for the rest of the day when I am finished."

Cordella nodded and offered Amira her hand.

The kind elder took Corvin from her. "He will be seen safely home. Don't worry for him."

Even as Cordella led her from the grove, Amira turned to see Corvin over her shoulder. She stumbled.

"Watch where you are going. He's in the elder's hands now."

"I hope I've not brought trouble down upon us by sending him back."

"No more than by taking him from his people to begin with," Cordella snipped.

10

POWER

"**C**ome on, we have a long walk up. The empty dwellings are far higher than where you stayed last night," said Cordella

"Can't we have the birds take us? They helped me before."

Cordella laughed, a fine tinkle of sound. "The birds only helped you because the elders asked them to."

"How did the elders know I needed help? I've never spoken to them until today."

"We could feel you, far from us. We all felt you, Amira."

"Oh. You can't talk to the animals?"

"Don't be foolish. The creatures of the Spindelskov do not speak."

"They spoke to me, all the way here."

Cordella's mouth fell open. "The creatures don't speak," she repeated, but quieter this time.

"Maybe they do and you just weren't listening."

"I don't think so." But Cordella didn't sound as sure as she had before.

They traveled back to the home trees in silence. Once they started up the tree, birds began to sing. A moth fluttered past and beetles scurried over the bark. A tiny lizard darted over the stair near her foot. Seeing them all gave Amira the courage to ask, "How do I dress like the rest of you?"

"You just dress yourself. How did you put on the clothes you wear now?"

"They were given to me by a maid. All my clothes were given to me. I don't know how to make them. Yours are made of leaves. How do you do that?"

"You ask the leaves to clothe you. Do you truly not know?"

Amira shook her head.

"What color do you like?"

"I often wore a green dress. It was one of the queen's favorites for me."

"Green is very simple. Let's start with that." She urged Amira to climb the stairs faster. Once they'd gone half as far up as they'd gone for the sun ceremony, Cordella stepped off the stairs and onto a platform that bridged over to a nearby tree. On that tree, she brought Amira to a dwelling twice as large as the one she'd slept in the night before.

"This one will be yours now. You will want to thank the tree so that it treats you kindly."

"How do I do that?"

Cordella let out a long sigh. "The elders owe me. I'm not a teacher."

"I'm sorry to be a bother."

"You'll need to put your hands on the trunk," Cordella said haltingly. "It's hard to explain all this. We just do it. It's very odd to think of one of us not knowing how."

Amira's eyes adjusted to the dim light inside the dwelling. The round edge of the trunk ran along one wall. She placed her hands on the rough surface. "Then what?"

"You talk to the tree."

"Like how I talked to the animals?"

"I suppose so?" Cordella sat on the floor. Her skirt puddled around her, making it seem like she floated and had no real legs at all.

Just before Amira pressed her palm against the tree, she paused. "What does the tree do for us?"

"Our trees keep us safe and provide all we need."

Amira didn't even know what all she needed, but it was clear Cordella's patience was wearing thin. Amira touched the tree and opened her mind like she'd done with the creatures who had traveled with her. The birds and mice had been better teachers.

A deep rumbling sound suddenly seemed to be laughing with her. "Small creatures have less will of their own, their minds are quiet, and hearts pure. It is in their nature to help others."

The tree spoke more than any of the creatures had. Its voice was much like her father's. Deep, patient, and she had the overwhelming feeling that it cared for all the Spindelkin.

"Thank you for helping me," she said. It seemed odd to be talking to a tree, something with no face, no eyes to peer into, nothing to indicate what it was doing or how it was feeling. The trees were so much bigger and older. Was she nothing more than a bird or mouse to them?

"More like a bear or a deer." The tree chuckled. "We care for all the creatures within our realm."

"I will do my best to care for you too."

The tree filled her with warmth. "You are tired. Go up and bask in the light. We will keep you safe."

Amira remembered how wonderful the sun had felt that morning, how beautiful it had been to be a part of all the Spindelkin, joined to them all even if it had only been for a few moments.

"Thank you, I will."

Amira took her hand from the tree and stepped away from the trunk. "I need to see the sun," she announced.

"I'll show you where I live and then you can make your way from there," said Cordella.

The two of them traveled up the tree along the winding stairs, walking over platforms where other dwellings circled the trunk. Branches seemed to rearrange themselves to allow the two of them clear passage upward. Birds swooped through the leaves, chirping merrily.

"This one." Cordella pointed to one of the two dwellings on the platform where they stood. They were starting to get narrower, following the width of the trunk.

Two children burst from the doorway and ran to greet Cordella.

"Where are you off to now?" asked a male voice as a man emerged a moment later. "Oh, you're home." He smiled at Cordella and then hugged her.

"Have you been aggravating your father again?" she glanced from one child to the other.

They shook their heads. Their hair hung just over their ears, and their faces and their height were near identical. The leafy tunics they both wore didn't offer any clues either. Amira stood aside and watched them together. It was the first Spindelkin family she'd seen together. The first family she'd seen together at all. While the king and queen had both visited her, they didn't visit at the same time. She'd only imagined whole families from the stories Father used to tell. They seemed very nice.

"This is Amira," Cordella said. "She's new to us and may have questions. If you see her, be kind with your answers."

The children nodded and so did their father. They were all staring at her.

"It was nice to meet you. I'll be on my way then." Amira put on her best calm smile and started up the stairs.

Once she was out of sight, she made a note of where Cordella's dwelling was so that she could find it again. She had a feeling that everyone knew these things and asking for directions was only going to make her the target of more stares.

She passed several other Spindelkin along the way to the top. They gave her clothing odd looks but went on their way without comment.

When she reached the platform where she'd been that morning with Cordella, there were only a handful of others there. She raised her face to the sun and let the warmth and light soak into her. No one was humming like they had that morning. The trees were quiet. Only the leaves and birds made noise.

"You're Amira?" asked a woman who suddenly stood beside her.

"Yes?"

Amira turned to face the older woman. Her hair hung long and loose, her skin cracked and pitted like an old tree. Whereas the elders had an aura of power, a strength about them, this woman was almost empty. She wore a simple dress of yellow leaves and not a single shining jewel.

"I am Cantazia."

Amira stilled. "My mother?" Even as she spoke the words, she knew the truth of them. That morning when she had been among all the Spindelkin she'd felt a part of them, one of them. But with Cantazia, they were two parts of the same thing, joined together.

The older woman nodded. "You feel it too?"

"The elders told me, but yes."

"We thought you were gone from us forever. We

couldn't feel you. No one could."

"I've been in Katra."

"You were stolen, my child." Cantazia's face softened. "I am glad you have returned to us. It gives me joy to look upon you before I give myself to the ground."

"What do you mean? Where is my father? Do I have brothers and sisters? Please, I've missed so much. Tell me."

Cantazia took Amira's hand and squeezed it. "You have been missed very much. You are the last of my children. The others are long grown and gone to their own families, most deep in the trees. Your father went with them to keep them safe. I have remained here in the hopes that one day what was stolen would be returned."

"I am free now, Mother. Please, tell me all about them, my brothers and sisters."

"Free now, yes. But were you returned?"

"I don't understand."

"Those that took you, did they see their error and see you safely back to us?"

"I escaped, Mother. The Queen of Katra did not wish to let me go. She threatened to burn Spindelskov if I left her."

Cantazia bared her teeth. "Our home will not be the one to burn. The very queen herself, you say? She will be punished, and all those who follow her. Thief."

"Please, Mother, there are kind people in Katra too. I would not see it burn. I am free now, isn't that enough?"

"You wear their clothes. You are a stranger to our

ways, a child who should be long grown by now. This queen has disturbed the order of nature. She is a thief. She must be punished."

11

WRATH

Amira's mother's threats gave her chills. Corvin was in Katra. She couldn't bear to have him harmed. Not after all she'd done to save him.

"Mother, I will stay here with you. You and the elders can teach me how to be a proper Spindelkin."

Cantazia ran her hand along Amira's cheek and smiled. "You are here and that brings me joy. But you are not the daughter I lost. You are part of them now, those that took you. I will speak to the elders in the morning."

"Will you spend this night with me and tell me about my family?"

Cantazia nodded. "We have missed a lifetime. One night is not too much to ask before I leave."

The sun and the trees, the elders, none of it mattered. She'd found her true mother. With her heart full, Amira led the way to her dwelling.

Cantazia walked inside and frowned. "My daughter,

you have nothing."

"I have a place to sleep." She pointed to the mat near the trunk of the tree. "What more should I have?"

Anger flowed from her mother, surrounding her with buzzing and snapping energy. "What kind of place did you come from that this is all you yearn for?"

"I had a big soft bed with many covers, baskets full of toys, and dresses as lovely as the Queen's. I lived in the castle, Mother." What she did not say was that her beautiful room was in the dungeon. Cantazia was angry enough. If Amira had any hope of talking her mother out of attacking Katra, some of the truth needed to remain silent.

Cantazia pointed at Amira's dirty nightdress. "This is what the queen of Katra wears?"

"I couldn't very well escape Katra in a fancy dress, Mother. They are heavy and not all that comfortable, especially for sleeping. The birds would have had a hard time carrying me."

"Birds carried you?" Cantazia shook her head. "I suppose you are still just a little slip of a thing. Katra's people did that to you, kept you a child. Kept you from the light, didn't they?"

"Yes, Mother." That was a truth she couldn't hide.

"Made you eat their food to confuse your body, to make it slow and weak."

"I didn't know any other way, Mother, or I would have refused to eat it."

Cantazia sat on the floor and beckoned Amira to

sit beside her. "I suppose you didn't. If you hadn't eaten, you would have faded away. They did keep you alive so you could return to us. For that, I will spare one life."

Only one? Amira's throat went dry. The king was a kind man. He didn't deserve the fate Cantazia intended for Katra. Jancy had helped her escape her room. She thought of all the maids locked in the dungeon, crying out for their freedom. And Corvin, innocent of all crimes, just a child.

"I would spare them all. Take the Queen if you must, but leave the rest."

"All? They knew you were one of us. They kept you from your people, the life you should have had. You were innocent, Amira, and now they have tainted you with their ways. You are weak and ignorant of what and who you are." Cantazia cocked her head, much like the bird who had spoken to Amira when she had first escaped the castle, listening, thinking. "What purpose would they have for taking you, one so young? You would never pass as one of them. The queen wasn't looking for a daughter."

A light grew within Cantazia, reminding Amira of how Cordella had glowed in the dark forest when they'd met. But this light wasn't soft and peaceful. It was bright and hot and lit red flecks in the depths of Cantazia's eyes. This was the Spindelkin of the stories, the terrifying creatures who lived in the forest, preying upon those who wandered too far inside.

"Mother, how is it that you glow?" Amira asked in the hopes of distracting her.

"You have no light inside? Have they taken this from you too?"

"I don't know," she said meekly.

Cantazia shook her head, her long hair rasping over the leaves of her dress. "One name, daughter. One life to be spared."

"Prince Corvin, the child who traveled with me."

"He is innocent enough." Cantazia nodded. "I will grant you this one life."

"Will you tell me about my family now?"

Cantazia made a growling noise. The light within her dimmed. She took Amira's hand in her own. "You had three brothers and four sisters."

"Had?"

"Time moves differently in the trees, little one. The deeper we go, the more different it is. Some may still live, but there are grandchildren and probably great-grandchildren I've never met. Your father undoubtedly went to ground some time ago. They traveled too far from me to feel them." She paused. "Do you know what the feeling is?"

Amira nodded. "I've felt it. Here, this morning up in the sun with the others, and very much with you."

"Good." Cantazia smiled. "Your father cared for the creatures of the forest. He could talk to them. He helped them and they in turn helped us. It was quite a rare gift."

"I can do that too."

"You can? That's wonderful." Cantazia squeezed her hand. "Now you know your place among us."

"I do?"

"I'm told one of the elders has elected to help you. He can explain."

Amira wished her mother would explain, that she would have more than one night with her. It seemed unfair that she'd found her real mother for such a short time, but it was better than no time at all.

They talked for hours until the only light in the dwelling was Cantazia's soft glow. When Amira couldn't keep her eyes open any longer, she went to her mat and stretched out.

"Good night, my daughter." Cantazia kissed Amira's cheek.

"Good night, Mother."

Cantazia left quietly, taking her light with her. In the peaceful darkness, with the knowledge of her family swimming in her head, Amira wondered just how different her life would have been if she'd never been taken from the Spindelskov. Certainly, the people of Katra would have been better off. She prayed Corvin, the king, and all the innocent people of Katra would be spared from the Spindelkin's wrath.

12

RAIN

Morning broke, the light reaching Amira's eyes and jolting her awake. She stretched and yawned and got up from her mat. The nightdress was dirty and wrinkled. Perhaps it was time she tried her hand at dressing like the Spindelkin.

She brushed her hand over the trunk of the tree. "How do I create clothing?"

"You have only to think and ask," said the tree in its slow pondering voice.

She thought of all the clothes the other Spindelkin wore, how they were fashioned, the colors, those that wore dewdrops like a rainbow of jewels, and others that adorned themselves with feathers, twigs, and stones. That seemed difficult for her first try. Instead, she thought of what she wore now, the simple nightdress, something she was comfortable in, that was easy for climbing the stairs, that wasn't heavy or cumbersome.

She didn't know which trees all the colors of leaves came from, the different shapes, and sizes. So she didn't think specifically, just green. Green would blend with the other leaves up above.

In the chill of the morning, she slipped out of the nightdress and rested her hand on the trunk of the tree. She thought hard of the green leaves and the shape of the nightdress she'd just stepped out of.

A stirring of winds swirled into the room. Amira turned away from the trunk to peer at the open doorway. Leaves blew in, one by one and then a handful, fluttering around her. Then another handful, and another, until she was so busy watching the leaves that landed on her, building one upon another that she lost track of the sheer number of them. Green leaves covered her skin in much the same way as the clothes she'd shed. Once the last ones gathered around her ankles into a loose skirt, she spun around taking in the weight and swirl of the leafy creation. They were soft and smelled of the clean breeze and sunlight. She tugged at one of them along the sleeve. It stayed in place, just as if it were sewn together, a fabric made of leaves.

She made sure to thank the tree and then dashed out of her dwelling. Amira all but ran up the stairs toward the top platforms where she could see others beginning to gather. Her mother would be there too. She couldn't wait to see her again, to show her that she'd been able to form clothes just like any other Spindelkin, that she was really one of them. She wasn't as tainted as her mother thought. All would be well.

When she reached the upper platform, she spotted Cordella standing with her family, but Cantazia was not to be found. Neither were the elders. Surely they need sunlight too?

Amira tried to stand patiently through the hand-holding and humming. The only moments she relaxed were when she, along with the others, raised their faces to the light.

A cloud passed overhead. Then another, until the entire sky was grey, shutting out the sunlight. If only the ceremony had begun a few minutes earlier, they might have finished. Now, the Spindelkin eyed the clouds and talked softly to one another. The young man holding her right hand leaned from the woman on his right to her.

"Rain is coming. We must return to our dwellings and conserve our strength until the sun comes again."

She nodded. He gave her an expectant look. Amira glanced at the man holding her left hand. He also seemed to be waiting. She leaned closer to him and repeated the message. By the time she had finished, she realized the chain of people on her right had dissolved. Spindelkin were filing down the stairs in an orderly line. She joined them.

The first drops fell, fat and wet. Rain splashed off the branches and made the steps slick. Each Spindelkin put one hand on the shoulder of the person in front of them. Joined together, they traveled downward. When they reached the dwelling levels, some dropped out of the line, but others moved forward to continue the chain. Amira's skin grew slick and her hair drenched, but everything under the cover of her leaf dress remained dry.

When the chain reached her platform, she almost dropped out of the line, but she wanted to find her mother. And was she still supposed to meet with the elder for her lesson even if it was raining? It seemed safest to go ask rather than hide away in her dwelling. Besides, she was already wet.

Amira continued on as the chain grew shorter and then she was alone. The family she left at the last platform gave her a strange look.

"I'm going to the glen," she said.

"Did you not hear the morning message?" asked the father.

"Yes, but I'm looking for my mother. Go, be dry." She shooed them toward the dwelling door.

Stepping carefully, Amira slowly made her way down the stairs. They were less wet the further down she went, the platform rings above offering some shelter. Once she reached the ground, she shook out her hair, squeezing water from the ends, and wove it into a quick braid like her maids had often done after her bath. It was much harder to do on her own, but her fingers quickly found the rhythm of it.

Amira looked around for something to tie around the end of the braid. The closest thing to a ribbon was a long, thin fern. She plucked a leaf and then tried to speak to it like she did with the trees. The fern had no voice, but she showed it a picture in her mind of what she needed it to do. Holding the fern near the end of her braid, it started to curl around it until it formed a tight roll. She thanked the fern and then continued on the path that many feet had formed from the stairway into the grove where she'd met with the elders the day before.

The tall rock wall had just come into sight when she heard voices. One was the angry elder who had wanted to cast her out. The other was her mother. Amira crept closer until she could make out other voices in the conversation. Though she couldn't make out all of the words, war, the queen, and Katra were all mentioned many times.

"Cantazia, we will vote. You have made your case. Go, and give us time to reach our decision," the loud elder said at last.

Cantazia stormed out of the grove, her hair wet and water splashing off her clothes. She nearly walked into Amira. Catching herself, she grabbed Amira's arm. "What are you doing here?"

"I came for my lesson with the elder."

"You shouldn't be here. Everyone is home, inside. Do you know nothing of weather or following rules?"

Her mother wasn't glowing exactly, not like the bright terrifying light she'd had the night before, but the red specks in her eyes were definitely there.

"I see you've at least made yourself some suitable clothing."

"Yes, mother."

Cantazia's face softened. "Green suits you nicely. It is good to see you dressed so."

Amira performed her best curtsy. "Thank you."

"Now, you should go rest. The rain came early this morning. Surely, you did not get your full sun."

"I slept all night. I'm fine. If the elder is willing, I will take my lesson."

"You are a strange girl." Cantazia let go of Amira's arm and shook her head. "I suppose you can wait here with me then. The elders are voting now."

They waited under the low branches of a nearby tree. Cantazia's lips quivered and her body shook the longer they stood there.

"What's wrong, Mother?"

"Are you not chilled by the rain?"

Amira shrugged. "It is no colder than the room where I lived. Rain is like having a bath."

"But you did not have full sun this morning." Cantazia looked her over, though what she was looking for was hard to tell.

"I lived for eleven years without seeing the sun. What little we did have this morning was plenty for me." She felt just as good as any other day. "What do you normally do when it's raining?"

"We sleep. It may rain for a short while or for days. We can only go so long without the sun so we rest and conserve our energy."

Amira couldn't imagine rain that lasted for days,

but she hadn't seen much other than sunny skies. "What about the elders? Don't they need to rest too? Why are they here and not in their dwellings?"

"The elders have lived a very long time, well past the years when most go to ground. It is said that they draw energy from the trees themselves."

"But the trees can't support all the Spindelkin, so most must get their strength from the sun," guessed Amira.

Cantazia smiled through her chattering teeth. "Exactly so."

"Why do you not ask the trees to help you on days like this one?"

"They have their own lives to look after. It would harm them to supply so many of us at once."

"Cantazia?" An elder called out.

"Yes?"

"Come, and bring the girl. We have heard both of you."

Amira followed her mother to the opening where the elders sat. The kind male elder smiled at her. The rest did not. She stood beside her mother and waited.

"We have decided," said a gnarled and hunched female elder, "to grant your request. You may take as many as will travel with you. The land that is now Katra must be cleansed. You will leave on the next sun."

"Thank you, elders." Cantazia grinned. She turned to Amira. "I will remember your request, daughter. If we do not meet again, know that it brought me great joy to see you with my own eyes."

"I am glad I got to meet you as well, Mother. Please come back safe." She kissed her mother's cold cheek.

13

HEALING

Cantazia left the clearing, arms wrapped around herself and hunched against the drizzle, leaving Amira alone in the gaze of all the elders.

"What business do you have here, little one?" asked the kind man.

"You said you would teach me."

"Today we have a war to plan. It is not a day for lessons. You should be in bed."

Tired of everyone telling her to go back to bed, Amira gave the elders a quick bow, like the maids did to the queen. That seemed to please them. Then she wandered back along the path. When she got to the stairs, the thought of spending all day in the little dwelling was like being in the dungeon. There was far too much to see and learn here. She had missed so much.

Amira wandered past the stairs, making sure to stay in a mostly straight line so she could find her way back. She walked to a mossy bed surrounded by low pink flowers. The soft, spongy moss felt wonderful on her feet. She curled her toes around the tiny, moist green fronds and smelled the sweet flowers.

"Not sleeping?" asked a small brown furry creature.

"I've not seen rain like this before. You're not sleeping either?"

"Rabbit," it said. "You scared my babies. We were resting just over there." The rabbit nodded to the underbrush beside the mossy circle.

"I'm sorry to bother you." Amira started to leave. "You speak much better than other animals I've talked with."

The rabbit's nose twitched. "Perhaps you are getting better at listening."

"Perhaps." Amira smiled at the rabbit.

The rabbit's back foot tapped. "If you could, one of my babies is ill. Can you help him?"

Cantazia and the elders had mentioned the Spindelkin having jobs in the forest. Her father had spoken to animals. Maybe this was her job. "I can try."

Amira followed the rabbit. There, tucked into a nest of fur, grass, and leaves, lay three tiny rabbits. Two picked up their heads and wriggled their noses at her. The third did not. It lay on its side, eyes closed.

She reached out slowly, watching the mother rabbit to make sure it was all right to do so. The rabbit did nothing to stop her. Amira sat down beside the nest and gingerly picked up the sick rabbit. It wasn't very warm, reminding her of how cold her mother had been in the rain. But the rabbit was dry.

As she had when she'd healed Corvin, Amira put one hand in the moss, letting her fingers sink into the velvety fuzz. She listened to the breath of the rabbit and that of the trees and plants around her, bringing the two together into one rhythm, in and out, breathing peacefully. Then she let the energy of the green things around her flow through her and into the little rabbit.

When she came back to herself, the rabbit was sitting up in her lap, blinking at her. She patted its soft, furry head, laughing at its twitchy little nose.

"Go on now, back to your brothers."

The little rabbit hopped from her lap and returned to the nest. The mother rabbit went over to sniff it. She returned to Amira.

"Thank you!" said the rabbit.

"I'm glad I could help. Farewell."

Amira continued on her path. Along the way, she came across other creatures. They were friendly enough but no one needed her help.

The rain finally let up. Rather than chance getting lost, Amira turned around and headed back to the city in the trees. She was just about back to the elder's grove when she spotted a large gathering of Spindelkin on the ground.

"What's going on?" she asked the nearest of them.

"We're marching on Katra. They stole one of us and now they must pay."

"Already? Don't you need to feed from the sun after

the rainy day?"

The young man looked at her oddly. "That was yesterday. We all saw the sun this morning. Surely, you were there? You look well."

"Yes, of course," she said, noticing the others wore more clothes than before. Some wore heavy-looking bark across their chests, others wore vests of tiny stones that were strung so closely together, they almost appeared solid. They all carried an array of spears and bows.

Time moved differently the deeper one went into the forest. They'd told her that, but she hadn't realized how differently in such a short distance. She'd only walked what seemed like half a day. Another hour or two would have brought her to the edge of the Spindelskov. For a moment she considered going with Cantazia's army.

She'd never seen fighting, with weapons or otherwise, but she'd heard stories. She wondered if she'd be able to talk with her mother and maybe convince her to punish only the queen, but she couldn't pick out Cantazia among them. There were too many people and some wore helmets of woven ferns or bark, making it harder to tell them apart.

"If you're coming with, you should choose your weapon." He pointed toward the scattered few spears that lay on the ground near the stairway.

"I'll do that, thank you." Amira made her way through the milling edges of the crowd. She didn't take a weapon, but she did climb up to the first platform. There, she walked out to the edge so she could better see the crowd.

Cantazia stood at the center with four of the elders. All of them wore helmets topped with white feathers. Someone blew a horn. The forest went still. The crowd began to form a line three people wide. It moved forward, snaking along until the first few rows were out of sight. One by one, Spindelkin joined the line. The sun had set by the time the crowd was gone.

Amira watched the trail they'd made in the fading light, hoping against hope that the Spindelkin might return, having changed their minds. But they didn't. The only consolation she discovered was that her skin now emitted a soft glow that was only visible when darkness settled in around her. At last, she was truly Spindelkin.

Slowly, as if she wore shoes made of stone, Amira made her way to her dwelling.

14

Travels

The next morning when Amira went to the sun ceremony, she was dismayed to find the upper platforms were near empty. She walked back down to the grove, but the remaining elders weren't there. Unable to receive any lessons and with most everyone gone to war, Amira grew restless. She sat in the quiet grove, waiting for the elders. As the sun arced overhead, she walked in slowly widening circles around the grove, looking for any sign of where they might have gone, but she found none.

Each day, after the sun ceremony, Amira watched the path the warriors had taken for any sign of their return. The plants grew back quickly and soon there was no sign of the path or the Spindelkin who had left. The tree city seemed wrapped in whispers, too quiet, too few kin left among the trees. And there was still no sign of the two elders who had stayed behind.

Hoping for news of her mother, Amira stayed close to the city. She sought out what animals she could find to practice speaking to them and offered any help she could.

Cordella approached her on the fourth day once the sun ceremony had ended. "Are you getting along well enough?"

"I suppose so. Where have the elders gone? I have not seen any of them since the army left."

"They went deeper into the trees to confer with those that dwell there. It's safer for them there in case Katra sends forces toward the trees."

"But you said the trees would protect us."

Cordella smiled. "They will, but it doesn't hurt to take precautions. Speaking of which, where have you been wandering off to?"

"I'm doing my job, but I'm not wandering far."

"Very good. Make sure you stay away from the border until the others get back."

"How long will they be gone?" Amira asked.

"We don't know. We haven't received any messages yet. I'm sure we will hear from them soon enough. Don't worry."

When Cordella left, Amira sat on her mat in her dwelling, wondering where her mother was and which elders had traveled with her. She hoped that the king was safe, and Corvin and all the others. But not all of them could be safe, not unless they had sat down to make a truce. Could they have done that? While she hoped that was the truth of it, her gut reminded her of how angry her mother had been and the unlikeliness of her sitting down to talk civilly with anyone from Katra.

That night, Amira dreamed of her bedroom in the castle. She played with the toys in the baskets and huddled under the warm covers. It was a simpler life there, only being worried about trying to get well and keeping the queen happy. She didn't have to worry about wars and the safety of the people she cared about or what side they might be on.

She wanted to speak to the elders, especially the one who had been kind to her. Surely, if they had sensed her in Katra before she'd come to the Spindelskov, they'd have news of some kind. The more she thought of the elders, a sense of unease settled over her.

Amira decided to take a trek deeper into the trees to look for the elders herself. If time really did move faster there, maybe by the time she returned, her mother would be home. She straightened her mat, and with nothing else holding her there, she went down to the ground and set out.

The farther she went, the closer together the trees grew. Towering trunks with tufts of green at the top loomed overhead. It was also darker here, but her glow helped light her way. She heard animals now and then, but none approached her. Hours passed with only the sound of her footsteps and the creaking of wood to keep her company. When she glanced up at the treetops next, there was no light.

Amira sank onto the spongy ground and pressed her back against a tree trunk. It was barely bigger around than she was. They were all like that here, at least those she could see in her glow.

While the light of the sun hadn't penetrated the darkness down on the ground, there was something uplifting, hopeful, about knowing that it was there. Even if it was out of reach. But now that it was gone, the darkness crept closer, cold and slithery. Fog rose from the ground and slipped around the trees to form a dense grey blanket. The fog dampened her glow further until she could only see a few inches from her fingers. It was almost as bad as when the candles went out in her room at night or when the maids ran late, leaving her with a guttering flicker before their arrival.

No one would be coming to light her way. Amira rested her hands on the trunk of the tree and opened her mind to it.

"It is so dark here," she said.

"Don't worry, little one. There are stars. You're just too small to see them."

A faint light caught her attention up above. As she watched, branches above her shifted, letting in a sliver of light from the moon and stars.

Amira patted the tree. "Thank you."

"Rest now, little one. You are tired."

She was. It didn't seem like it should be night already, but the moon didn't lie. A blanket of leaves crept over her until she was comfortably warm.

Amira traveled for six nights, each coming faster than the one before it. Though the trees changed kinds and some spots had hills and others had sandy soil that shifted under her feet, the trunks remained tall and thin. Each morning the tree she slept under parted its leaves so she could take in the sunlight.

How far could the next tree city be? It was lonely out here with no one to talk to, not an irritable queen, a scared maid, or even a fellow Spindelkin to give her an odd look. She did see an occasional animal, but none came close enough to speak to.

As she walked, she realized her dress had grown tight and shorter than it had been. She hadn't noticed any leaves falling off. Amira held out her hands. Were they bigger? She couldn't be sure. Her hair was longer. How much time had passed, she wondered.

After making sure no one was around, she shed her too-small dress and asked the nearest tree to gather up leaves to make a new one. Once the breeze and flurry of leaves had subsided, she looked down. The new dress was much the same as the old, but these leaves were darker green, some with veins of golden yellow.

"Thank you," she said to the tree. "Your leaves are lovely."

The tree sent her a burst of warmth. Amira returned it and then continued on her way.

She was almost ready to turn back two very short days and nights later when she finally saw someone.

"Welcome," said a girl no taller than her waist. "You

must be new here. I don't know you."

"I am. Thank you." Amira smiled. "How far is it to the others?"

"Just over the hill. I'm not supposed to go any farther than this. I'm waiting for my friend."

"Have fun with your friend." Amira left the girl and walked up the hill.

On the other side, the sun shown down brightly. She ran toward it. While the trees had given her enough sun to get by on her travels, she now realized just how much she missed being surrounded by the light. She ran into the pool of sunlight and raised her face to bask in the warmth. A soft flow of energy filled her in places she hadn't realized were near empty.

Once she was finally full, she took the time to look around. This city seemed smaller than the one she'd come from. A circle of trees formed a ring around an opening in the leafy canopy. A stream ran through the middle with flowers and tall grass on both banks. Butterflies danced above the water and landed on mossy rocks at the edge. The tree bearing the stairs upward lay on the other bank. She looked for a safe place to cross.

Other Spindelkin traveled from one side to the other using a thick log. She followed them across. They nodded to her but didn't speak. She missed the little girl who had seemed happy to talk to her.

Was she supposed to ask someone for permission to go up the stairs? She didn't know anyone and she didn't see the elders. Surely they must have also traveled here?

"Are you looking for a dwelling for the night?"

Amira spun around to see a man with a long beard. He wore tiny bones woven into three long braids that hung down his chest. His clothing was a similar green to her own.

"Yes. I've just arrived. I came to see the elders that traveled here from Gorsia."

"They are in our grove. I can take you there."

Amira nodded. "That would be most helpful."

"I'm Gorm," he said as they walked beyond the stair tree and away from the sunlight.

"Amira." She glanced over her shoulder, wishing she could go back and just sit in the light until the sun went down. She'd been too long in the darkness.

"Your elders spoke of you. We were not told that you would be coming."

"What did they say?"

He gave her a dark look. "That there will be war because of you. There are already too few of us."

Her feet refused to move. "Because of me? I was stolen. I asked for no war. That was the choice of my mother and our elders."

"But it is because of you."

She did not like the sound of that at all. This was none of her doing.

"I would see the elders now," she said stiffly.

Gorm pointed through the tall bushes they'd come to. "They are down the path, through there."

15

BETRAYAL

Amira left Gorm and walked through the bushes. She couldn't hear the voices of the elders, not like in the other grove. But there didn't appear to be any large rock walls or many rocks at all. There were no echoes here.

The bushes grew close together, making it difficult to wade through. Leaves formed a dense ceiling overhead. Still, she heard no sign of the elders.

She walked further until it grew so dim that her skin began to glow. She'd had plenty of darkness on her way here. The circle of sunlight she'd passed through called to her. Amira turned around and considered going back. The light had felt so good. Like she'd been clean, fresh from a long, warm bath. The air in this grove was cool and damp. When she finally did hear something, it wasn't voices, but the rushing of water over rocks. The stream that ran under the log bridge wound through the trees. While the stream grew wider, the path narrowed.

Amira found herself at the water's edge. The path seemed to end there. Surely, the elders wouldn't have traveled this way. She couldn't imagine them jumping over the stream.

She glanced over her shoulder, confirming that she'd not missed a branch in the path or elders tucked away somewhere. Gorm had sent her this way and he had no reason to lie about the elders being here. Maybe she just hadn't gone far enough yet. Maybe the elders had a way to get over the stream that she'd missed. Amira squared her shoulders, judged the distance to the far bank, and took a running leap.

Her bare feet sunk into the black muck but she kept her balance. Mud squished between her toes for the first few steps. The leaves made quick work of wiping the grime away as she pushed her way forward on the narrow trail.

A grunting noise made her heart race. A moment later, a brown bear ambled from the trees to stand in her path. Amira froze.

The bear watched her for a moment, sniffing the air. Then it rose on its hind legs and let out a growl that made Amira's stomach drop to her feet. Its paws ended in giant claws as long as her fingers. The bear growled again, then dropped to all four feet and ran at her, head swinging back and forth, its sharp teeth clear even in the dim light.

Run, she thought to herself. And she tried. But her

feet had forgotten how to move. All she could do was hold out her hands in front of her, as though that would keep the giant beast away.

"Why are you angry with me?" she cried.

The bear's wet nose rubbed against her cheek as it sniffed her. Its rancid breath made her ill. "Food?"

"I'm not food," she said. "Why are you angry?"

The bear took a step back and looked at her. "Hungry."

"What do you eat?"

The bear showed her pictures in her mind: berries, mushrooms, bugs, and yellow flowers.

"Why are these things not here for you?"

"Hungry," it said again.

"I will help, but you must wait here and not eat me."

The bear sniffed her again, taking great puffing breaths and blowing them in her face. "Wait?"

She nodded.

The bear sat. Its giant claws dug into the ground where it rested its weight on them. It watched her intently.

Amira did her best to block out the giant, hungry bear that wanted to eat her so she could concentrate. She reached out to the bushes all around her. They were tired, not getting enough light. Everything here was so dark.

She walked among the bushes, finding them able to bear the fruits the bear wanted. But they needed light, and then they would need her help. The more she reached out to the plants all around her, she found them all to be weary and unable to grow as they should.

Touching the nearest tree, she spoke to it. "Why do you keep all of the light from everything below?"

"The ground is so far down and we cannot see what is there. We have not been tended to in a long time."

"But the lack of light is hurting the other plants and the animals that need to eat from them."

"Where are your people? They are not tending to the forest as they should."

"Gorm said there weren't enough kin. I will do what I can to help. Please spread your branches."

The tree was a long time in answering. "Very well."

Branches moved overhead, rearranging themselves until sunlight filtered down to the ground where she stood.

"Thank you," she said to the tree.

She went from one tree to the next, making the same request until she grew tired from the effort of speaking to the slow-moving trees. At least there was light here now, but even that was fading as the sky grew orange and red.

"We will sleep," she said to the bear. "If you keep me warm, I will feed you tomorrow."

"Agreed."

Amira sat down next to the bear. It was warm, and she had no doubt that it would keep her safe for the night. After all, it would protect its food. She only hoped she could convince the bushes to make berries in the morning or she might become bear food herself.

Sleeping next to a bear brought a host of problems. The foremost of which was that the bear snored. Loudly. All night. And it stunk like a week-old chamber pot. And no matter how hard Amira tried to sleep, she kept smelling it. What little sleep she did get would have to be enough.

Morning came with a burst of warm light from above. Sunlight brought both a sense of relief and trepidation. Now she had to make food for the bear or face the consequences.

"Food?" asked the bear as it watched her with its beady dark eyes and bared its sharp, yellow teeth.

"I'm trying."

Amira took a deep breath. She stood in the sun, trying to get as much light as possible. She let the light soak in and then reached out to the bush next to her. Sharing the urge to live and thrive with the bush, she coaxed it to make more leaves, to make them bigger to capture all the light it could. Then she asked it to make berries.

One by one, small green balls formed on the ends of the tiny branches. With her help, they grew bigger, and then slowly a bright red wash of color crept over each one until they were ripe. She pulled back from the bush, slowing the growth so the berries didn't fall off or rot.

"Now," she told the bear, but as soon as she said that, she felt the bush shy away. "Wait."

Amira knelt next to the bush and gently picked the

berries. She gathered them into a pile in her skirt and then sat beside the bear.

Filling her hand with ripe berries, she held them out, trying not to shake. "Now you can eat."

The bear gobbled them up, his wet tongue rasping over her palm and tickling her fingers. He kept his teeth to himself. Amira sighed with relief as she fed it the rest of the berries.

"More," the bear begged with sullen eyes.

Her search for the elders would have to wait until the bear was full. She couldn't very well have a hungry bear follow her back to the other Spindelkin or the elders if she could find them.

With a heavy heart, Amira spent the day and all of the next, bringing the plants that grew under the trees back to health. A skinny rabbit poked its head out of one of the bushes and nibbled at the leaves. A bird sang overhead. The bear, with its stomach finally full, ambled off into the dark forest.

Exhausted, Amira dropped down onto the ground and fell against one of the trees.

"Wake," a slow voice said in her head.

Amira came awake quickly and sprang to her feet. She couldn't see anyone around. Leaves rustled overhead.

"You have done well here, but you must go," said the tree she'd fallen asleep against.

"Why?"

"Other Spindelkin are coming. The trees have seen this."

"Other Spindelkin? I wish to speak with them. That's why I came."

The tree was gone from her mind for a long moment before it returned. "They have learned that the bear did not eat you."

Had Gorm wanted the bear to eat her? She couldn't imagine such a thing. He had seemed angry with her, but the war wasn't her fault. If the other Spindelkin in this city felt the same way, she wasn't safe here.

Amira considered where to go. It was a long way back home and she still needed to find the elders, if not those from this city, those that had traveled from Gorsia. She just needed to avoid Gorm's people for a little while.

Amira reached out to the creatures nearby, touching their minds until she found one that suited her needs. A stag crept out from the trees.

"Would you mind carrying me? I may need to get away quickly."

The stag knelt, allowing her to get on its back. "We will stay near, but out of sight for now."

He stood and picked its way through the half-dead underbrush. They hung back in the dim light. Amira hoped it was enough to mask her faint glow.

Three Spindelkin, wearing armor just like the army that had left for Katra, came into the healthy clearing she had made. They turned around, taking in all the changes.

"The bear failed," said a woman. "At least the troublesome girl has been busy."

"I thought you said you had a deal with the bear,"

said a tall man wearing yellow leaves.

"I did," said Gorm. "It was hungry. She was food. I thought I was pretty clear."

"Where did she go?" asked the woman.

The three of them split up, eyeing the ground and slowly wandering the entire space. "I found footprints. A deer."

"What about hers?"

"There's sign of her, but with all the leaves, it's hard to tell where exactly. I don't see that she's left. Do you?"

The other two shook their heads.

"You know what we must do. We're close. Are you sure you're able?" asked Gorm.

Again the other two nodded.

"Good. That little female has brought enough trouble on our fellow kin. Sending them off to a war they can't win," Gorm said. "The forest is already sorely neglected, this will ruin us all. She must pay for what she's done."

The man in yellow leaves grunted. "I can't believe Gorsia's elders agreed to war."

"Gorsia's elders were foolish, swayed by the words of the girl's mother. The girl shouldn't have been welcomed among us. She's tainted by the ways of men."

"Our forest suffers for lack of those to tend it and she thinks to heal trees here? What of those surrounding Gorsia? They will suffer far worse?" asked the woman.

"She claimed ignorance, but I don't believe her," said Gorm. "Katra's queen likely sent her back to us to stir up this war, to flush us from the trees, to drive us out under the open skies to die."

Amira shuddered. What Gorm was saying couldn't be true. Cantazia would come home. All of the kin would. Surely.

The man in yellow said, "You were right to hold Gorsia's elders. They should be punished just as much as the girl."

Punishing her meant feeding her to a bear? Amira held on tight to the stag who stood silently in the shadows of the dense leaves. The elders were in danger too. She had to find them.

Amira leaned close to the stag's ears and whispered, "Can you please take me back to the city where these kin came from?"

The stag watched the armed kin warily and then picked his way around the clearing with delicate steps.

"What's that?" asked the woman, peering into the trees. "I thought I saw a glow."

"A deer, by the sound of it," said the man in yellow.

"She's riding the deer! After them!" yelled Gorm.

The deer didn't need to be told what they were saying. It bolted off through the underbrush and between the trees at a speed that drove Amira to cling to its neck. She kept her head down and pressed against his fur, safe from the wide spread of antlers and branches that threatened to grab her as they ran.

The footsteps of the kin chasing them quickly fell behind. The deer did not slow down. It bolted all the way back to the stream, leaped across it, and ran down the path she'd followed.

When she spotted the hill, she asked the stag to stop. His sides heaved and warm steam unfurled from his nose.

"Go and be safe." Amira leapt from the stag and dashed toward the nearest set of stairs. She had to find the elders before Gorm and the others found her first.

16

RESCUE

Two children sat on the first platform Amira came to, singing a song as they clapped each other's hands.

"You're the new kin," said the little girl she'd met before.

"Yes. I need your help. Did you see two elders arrive here before I first did?"

The girl nodded. "They're up top. They were bad."

"Where? Can you show me?"

The girl looked at her friend.

"Mom will be mad. We're not supposed to go by the bad people," said the other little girl.

"They're not bad," said Amira. "Please. We need to hurry."

"Why are you all dirty?" asked the first girl.

The other one wrinkled her nose. "And you smell bad."

"I've been working. Helping a bear."

The girls again looked at one another and shrugged.

"I'll show you where the elders are, but you can't tell anyone," said the first girl.

"I promise."

That seemed to appease them. The two girls ran to the stair tree and up they went. Amira walked behind them, her strides eating up two of theirs. It wasn't until she'd seen Gorm mostly eye to eye that she realized she was full-grown now. Whether it was the time changes on her travel through the forest or working with the trees and animals, her body had finally caught up to where she guessed it was supposed to have been for her age. Her dress was again too small and tight.

Around and around they went, one platform after another and a bridge to one tree and then the next. Amira had been so busy following the girls that she had no idea how to go about getting back down again. At least she had a head start on Gorm and the others, but if she couldn't get back down, she didn't know how she'd be of any help to the elders once she found them.

"They're in there," said the friendly girl. She pointed to a platform on the next tree. It lay across a bridge with a closed door on the dwelling.

Amira had never seen a door on one of the dwellings before. It didn't appear to have a knob or any sort of handle like the doors in the castle.

"How do they get out?"

"The tree has sealed them in."

"Because they're bad," said the other girl.

"They're going to be punished."

"Punished how?" asked Amira.

The friendly girl beckoned her down so she could whisper, "The dwelling shrinks a little each day. Soon the tree will eat them and they will become one with the tree."

While that sounded terrifying, Amira wondered if the Spindelkin were even more frightened of the darkness and being shut in the dwelling. She doubted they'd ever been stuck in a pitch-black room before, with the door locked, and not knowing if someone was going to ever open it.

She didn't want them to suffer like that, not knowing. And she certainly didn't want them to be eaten by the tree.

"Thank you for your help. You can go now so you don't get in trouble."

"Be careful," said the friendly girl.

The two of them darted off.

The few Spindelkin she spotted watched her. She gauged how far away they were and how long it would take her to get across the bridge. None of them appeared to be armed. A ruckus sounded far below. People were yelling. She peered downward only to see others pointing up to where she was.

Amira ran across the bridge, heedless of the swaying, eyes only on the dwelling ahead. She reached the other side and knocked on the door. it still sounded hollow.

A knock answered her.

The elders were alive.

Amira darted around the dwelling until she found a spot to wedge herself into where she could touch the trunk of the tree.

"Please, you must open up and let them out."

The tree didn't answer.

She tried again, pushing her thoughts into the tree.

"The elders have spoken," the tree finally answered.

"These are elders. Please, let them free."

"The elders have passed judgment. We will do as they ask."

"No. You must not. I haven't seen elders here. There may not be any. Either way, you are being fooled."

"Fooled? What is this?"

Amira backed away from the tree and gathered the sunlight into her, refilling her energy as much as she dared in a quick minute. Then she again rested her hand on the rough bark.

"I have searched but found no elders. Was it Gorm who told you to punish these elders?"

"Yes," said the tree in a long, slow breath.

"He is no elder, only an angry kin. The elders you hold within you came only to be safe. They caused no harm. Please, my kin from Gorsia need these elders back. I need them. The Spindelskov needs them."

"In that, you are right, little one." The tree heaved a sigh. "We must learn if what you say is true."

"How will you learn? I don't have much time. Gorm and his followers are after me."

"I will speak to the other trees."

The shouts grew louder. Footsteps beat their way up the stairs. A few kin who were coming down from above, paused to peer at her and the chaos rising up from below.

"Please speak quickly."

The tree went silent.

Gorm and the two who had been with him marched onto the platform across the bridge. Ten other men and women joined them. Other kin gathered on the platforms above and below in the trees around her.

"We're out of time," she whispered.

"Now who is foolish?" The tree quaked.

There was a popping noise and suddenly the end of the bridge connected to the side where she was, fell free. The bridge swung down, nearly hitting several kin who stood on the platform below on the connected tree. The kin scattered.

"You have asked trees to let light in?"

"Yes. They were keeping light from reaching the ground. Animals were starving. Plants were dying."

"No kin have served that part of the forest in many seasons," observed the tree.

"Please, you cannot afford to lose more Spindelkin. There are too few of us to serve all the trees."

"You speak the truth," said the tree.

The wood covering the door shook and shivered. A

hole opened, only the size of her fist. A weathered face pressed to it.

"Amira?"

She ran to the hole. "I'm here."

"How?"

"No time for that. Talk to this tree, explain why you are here and why you must be set free. Show it that you are elders and that Gorm is not."

"We've tried. It won't speak to us."

"It will now. Do it. Hurry."

She leaned against the dwelling, keeping her eyes on Gorm and the others. Two more men shouldered their way through the growing crowd. They carried bows.

"They are going to shoot us," she told the tree. "Hurry."

"The kin would never harm a tree."

An arrow arced through the air. Amira wasn't about to let it hit her just to spare the tree learning that the kin were about to do what it said they never would. She dodged aside, running to the back of the dwelling.

The arrow thunked into the wood side of the dwelling.

The tree let out a jolt that shook the platform.

Another arrow hit the dwelling just beside where she stood. Amira spun around to see other kin with bows on the platforms all around her.

"You must help me," she said to the tree.

The tree shook. An angry energy built up all around her. Amira realized it was coming from the tree itself. The door to the dwelling cracked open. The elders huddled inside.

"What is happening?" they asked.

"The kin are firing arrows at me and hitting the tree. I think it's very angry."

The kind elder pressed his forehead to the tree and closed his eyes.

The other beckoned her within the safety of the dwelling walls. "You have learned much and quickly, Amira. Perhaps one day, you will be an elder, but you are young, with much life to live first, I think."

The kind elder pulled away from the tree just as another arrow struck the wood. "We must stop this," he said. "If we don't, the trees here will turn against their kin and destroy them."

Amira thought of the little girl and her friend. Some of the kin here were up to no good, but the forest needed all of them. Perhaps the elders could set Gorm and the others straight on the way of things.

The tree shook again.

Amira glanced around the clearing and spotted birds flying high above them all. She called to them.

"Take the bows from their hands. Be careful. They are harming the trees and may hurt you too."

The birds came as one, a giant flock swarmed down upon the kin with bows. They clawed at the weapons and buffeted the faces of the men with their wings. One by one, the bows fell to the ground or were carried away by the birds.

"Thank you, little one," said the tree. "You are free to go. These kin will be dealt with."

"Be gentle with them," she said. "You need them as much as they need you."

"You are wise. It will be so."

A long branch swooped down from above, wrapping itself around one of her elders. It took him down to another branch, which in turn carried him down to another. Another one grabbed her and carried her downward. By the time she reached the ground, the first elder was already there, and the other was only a branch away.

Both of the elders stood hunched lower than they'd been before, their skin even more winkled. Just as she'd aged on her journey here, so had they.

"We must return to Gorsia," Amira said. "The forest must be healed."

"It is a long journey," said the kind elder. "We may not make it back again. When we found no elders here, we'd planned to stay for what little time we have left."

"Then you will travel as far as you can. I need to learn so much yet and you said you would teach me."

Amira called for help from the animals. A small herd of elk answered. The elder's eyes grew large as the elk approached them.

"Get on, quickly," Amira urged. "They will help us move faster so that you might reach Gorsia."

Their elderly bodies had difficulty getting onto the elk, but it was patient and with Amira's assistance, they managed. Once the three of them had mounted, the elk trotted into the trees.

They traveled for many days and nights, stopping to stretch their muscles and backs to talk for a short while before they slept. When the days began to grow longer, Amira knew they were almost home. She hoped to find her mother and the others had returned and that all was well with the forest.

17

GORSIA

The grove where the elders had first met with her was quiet. The ferns had grown thick in the place where they'd sat.

Amira thanked the elk for their help. The great horned beasts loped away and disappeared into the shadows.

"Wait here," she said to the elders. "I'll get closer and see what there is to see. We don't want to get put in a tree again."

The elders seemed grateful for the chance to sit on something that wasn't moving. They were old before, but now they seemed ancient.

"We'll be fine here, go on," said the elder, waving her off.

Amira crept closer to the village in the trees. No one called out. She could see a few people moving, but everything seemed so quiet. Even the birds were hushed here.

She worked her way halfway up the stairs until she finally met someone.

A young man looked her over, his brows drawing together. "Who are you?"

"My name is Amira. I was here before for a short time."

"I don't remember you."

"That's not surprising, everyone was busy gathering to leave for the attack on Katra."

His mouth dropped open. "Katra? I was a child when my father left to attack Katra. How old were you?"

"I'm not sure. Eleven? I went after the elders who went deeper into the forest. I brought them back."

"You brought elders? Thank the trees. We haven't had elders here for so long." He glanced around and stepped closer, talking quietly. "Not real ones. Four adults named themselves elders and have been telling everyone what to do, but they can't talk to the trees like real elders do."

"Why not? Everyone can talk to the trees," she said.

"Yes, we can talk to them, but they choose whether to answer or not. They listen to elders."

"Ah, I see the difference. The elders are in the grove now. Hopefully, they will start talking to them soon then. The trees must miss them."

He nodded. "Did you know my mother, Cordella?"

"Oh yes! She was my guide here. I met you when you were a child." Amira paused. "Wait, does that mean I'm old now?”

He smiled. “You’re an adult but you don’t look old.”

“Thank goodness. I wasn’t gone that long.”

“They say the forest cares for those that care for it.”

Amira peered upward through the leaves. “Where is everyone? Your parents?”

Sorrow crossed his face. “My father never returned. No one did. Once my sister and I were grown, my mother went to ground. She was very sad.”

“No one returned? My mother was with them too.” Amira remembered the Queen’s threats. “There wasn’t a fire, was there?”

He shook his head. “If there was, it never reached this far into the trees.”

“That’s very good to hear. I’m sorry about your parents.”

“No one knows what happened outside the Spindelskov. The lookouts won’t go to the edge of the forest. They say it’s cursed now, that everything that was out there has changed.”

Amira had the sudden urge to see the changes for herself. “I will sleep here with these trees tonight and tomorrow, I will go to the edge of the Spindelskov and see what became of our people.”

“You are very brave,” he said.

The king used to tell her that too. She wondered if he was still in his country estate or if he’d gone back to live at the castle with the queen. And what of the baby she’d returned?

"There are many homes open. Most of us live up near the top now," he said.

"I'll stay here, out of the way then. Thank you."

"I hope you'll join us for the sun ceremony before you leave."

Amira remembered the first one that she'd ruined with Corvin's cries. "Thank you, but I shouldn't. I don't live here anymore. And besides, the last time I tried to fit in here, most of our people went to war and didn't return."

He nodded sadly and wished her well before taking the spiraling stairs upward. Amira returned to the elders in the grove to tell them what she'd learned.

She entered the grove and searched the dappled light for the old men she'd left there, but they were gone. She ran around the rocks, the trees, the ferns, searching. No white hair, no long beards, no friendly faces. What had happened to them? Had Gorm's people from deep in the forest followed them and taken the elders back or done them harm?

Scared, she reached out to the nearest tree, placing her hand on the rough bark. "Where did the elders go?" she asked the tree.

Clouds crossed the sky and insects buzzed around her head before the tree answered. "They earned their place amongst us. Thank you for bringing them back."

"But where are they?"

"Look, little one."

A single yellow leaf drifted down from above. It

came to land on the mossy ground next to two tiny saplings that had sprung up next to the rocks where she'd last seen the elders.

She thanked the tree and went to sit next to the tiny saplings. "I'm sorry I missed you leaving. I didn't get to say goodbye." She touched the stick-like trunk of one of the tiny trees and the five freshly unfurled green leaves atop its single branch.

While the little tree did not speak, she could feel it smiling at her. "Be well and grow tall," she said to the two saplings before returning to the stairway to find shelter for the rest of the day and night. A good long sleep sounded like just the thing she needed before leaving on another journey.

She settled into the first dwelling she found on the lowest platform. As she lay on her back, staring at the wooden ceiling, she thought back to what the tree in the grove had said. Us. Were all the trees in the grove grown from old elders? All the trees? All of the Spindelskov?

Amira reached out to the trunk of the tree that served as home for Gorsia. "Are the trees and the kin one and the same?"

"Yes, little one. We are all the same. One day, you too will stand tall and strong. Now, sleep. You have much to do before it will be your time to join us."

Amira closed her eyes. She missed the warmth of an animal, even the stink of the bear, the elders' snores, Corvin's soft breathing, her mother's voice. For a moment, she felt very alone, but then she realized the trees were all around her, that her very dwelling was part of the one she'd been speaking with. Comforted, she drifted off to sleep.

When she woke, sunlight shown into the doorway, beckoning her. Amira waited for her eyes to adjust outside the shelter before taking in the forest around her. If she was going to set out on a new journey, it was time for fresh clothing. She couldn't march into Katra in the dress she wore now, its leaves torn and fading. These leaves had served her well. They'd earned their rest on the forest floor where they would become one with the soil. Stepping back into the privacy of her dwelling, she released the leaves she'd worn. They fell to the floor with a soft swoosh, leaving her skin bare and chilled. If she was going to go to Katra to find her people, or what had become of them, she was going to dress for the part. The queen had always insisted she dress for her station.

Amira thought of the queen's gowns and realized none of them would be suitable for walking through the forest. They were meant for large open spaces in the castle where not much walking was required. Perhaps, she considered, it would be better to dress for the journey rather than the destination. She could always change at the edge of the forest.

In a sensible green dress, Amira set out. What did her mother's army do to the queen? Was little Corvin safe and growing strong? Wondering what she'd find in Katra, Amira hurried onward. She passed trees she recognized, but there was no sign of the army that had left Gorsia, even for the size that it had been. The kin had left no mark on the forest. Then again, she'd been gone so long that Cordella's son had grown into an adult. The forest had likely long ago grown over whatever trail the kin had left behind.

The sight of green-needled trees told her she was nearing the edge of the Spindelskov. The tall trees dropped away behind her, allowing her a better view of the blue sky full of white clouds. The field that had stood before the forest was no longer a field. Trees grew throughout the tall, lush grass. They stood half as tall as the Spindelskov, their branches reaching upward, their leaves blowing in the soft wind. The scattering of trees spread as far as she could see. Bright flowers merrily dotted the deep green grass. The flowers were of all kinds, but so many were lilies, like the one that had sprouted from the floor in her bedroom in the castle. Where the drop of her blood had spilled.

Amira stood in the waving field of flowers surrounded by the trees that had been her people and wept.

A terrible war had happened here. If any of the people of Katra had died, there was no sign of them. When she'd run out of tears, Amira took a deep shuddering breath and set off toward Katra.

18

THE TOWER

Each step brought her closer to the life she'd escaped from.

Butterflies landed in her hair. Rabbits hopped along beside her. For most of the afternoon, a field mouse rode on her shoulder. Throughout her walk, Amira was never alone. By early evening, she passed beyond the last of the trees of her fallen people. As the sun set and a chill settled in the air, a wolf loped out of the growing shadows to keep her company. She tried to speak to it, but it didn't seem to understand. She realized none of the animals she'd seen during the day had spoken.

Confused, she watched the rising moon and wondered what the next day would hold.

On the second day of her travels through the meadowlands, Amira spotted a tall, thick tower made of grey stone. It hadn't been there when she'd first traveled to the Spindelskov.

Three men in armor stood on the open top of the tower. One pointed at her. The other two ran to his side. They stood, watching. She guessed they were speaking, but she was too far away to hear their voices.

One of the men lit a torch and held it high, waving it around in a big circle. The giant door at the bottom of the tower opened. A man on a horse rode out. Two more followed, riding in single-file. The door closed behind the last one. They wore shiny armor and carried swords at their sides. They rode straight for her.

Birds began to swarm overhead, chittering louder and louder until she could barely hear herself think.

The three men on horseback drew up close. The horses were much taller than her, and the men on their backs even more so. For all her growing up, she still was small compared to the people of Katra.

The men all wore helmets. The one in the front bore a red plume. With all the armor, she couldn't see much of his face or body. He was all metal but for narrowed eyes that weren't at all friendly, a long nose with a little bump in the middle, and a pair of downturned lips. His helmet covered him to his chin and above his eyebrows. He said something, but the birds were too loud. The other two men clapped their gloved hands, making a racket of their own. The birds were not impressed.

Realizing she was never going to get anywhere with all the noise, Amira thanked the birds for their warning. Still, they did not cease.

"Enough," she yelled.

The birds went silent, their tight circle loosening, but still swirling over her head.

The three men on their horses stared down at her with wide eyes. The red-plumed man recovered first.

"Go back to your cursed forest. Your kind are not welcome here," he said.

"My kind was killed here. I wish to know why and speak to any that remain."

The man drew his sword. The other two spread out, moving on either side of her.

"Your kind stole our prince eighteen years ago. They were dealt with without mercy for stealing a defenseless child."

So long? Amira pointed to the trees who had been her kin. "I was also a defenseless child and your queen stole me. Did they also not have the right to deal with you in the same manner?"

"How dare you speak of the Queen that way." He swung the sword, but before the blade could reach her, his horse shied away. The other two horses danced backward.

Though Amira hadn't asked the horses to help her, she thanked them.

"I would like to speak to your queen, who once called herself my mother."

"The queen never would have let a monster like you into her family," snarled the man.

"Let's discover the truth of that together." Knowing that the queen was alive, Amira looked forward to making the people of Katra understand just who she was and what had been done to her to give them the golden fields they worked in and the lush gardens they ate from.

"The prince, is he well?"

"Well enough. He's at the tower. I'm sure Prince Gerald would love to get the chance to talk to you after what your kind did to ours."

Disappointment flooded through her. Of course the queen would give him a different name. Would the prince remember her? Amira glanced toward the Spindelskov, wishing she could go back and ask the trees for advice. However, the men around her did not appear the patient sort.

Birds spun in lazy circles overhead, creating shuttered shadows with their wings. Something here wasn't as it should be. Why weren't the animals speaking? And if the prince was near, wouldn't it be nice to see him again, even if he wasn't the baby she'd sent back to his mother?

"I would like to speak to the prince." Maybe he would have the answers she sought. It would be far better to talk to him than to face the queen. After seeing so many new trees and knowing the reason for them, she wasn't ready for that yet.

"Follow me," said the guard, urging his horse forward with the nudge of his knees.

The other two fell into place behind her, making her feel like she needed to rush along. The horse's legs were as tall as she was, making the men upon them seem like giants. While she didn't mind the trees being impossibly tall, the men made her uneasy. The only thing that kept her nerves in check was that the horses themselves appeared to be on her side, even if they didn't speak to her.

The walk was long and the men were impatient with her short steps, but she hurried as much as she was able. By the time they reached the tower, she was out of breath, her sides heaving and mouth dry.

"Might I have some water?"

"Inside," the guard said, motioning to the men on top, who yelled to someone behind the walls.

The great door creaked open. Inside, pigs, goats, and chickens wandered about between the legs of eight other horses who stood behind a fence. Other men in armor stood inside, watching her with mostly-averted eyes. No one but the red-plumed guard spoke to her.

"There, if you're thirsty." He pointed to a long wooden box on the ground that was half-filled with murky water.

A goat went over and drank from it. She decided she wasn't that thirsty. Even the animals deserved cleaner water than that. "I'll wait, thank you."

The guard shrugged. "Suit yourself." He slid off his horse as did the men who had ridden with him. "Wait here."

Without any further instruction, she was left standing in the middle of the courtyard with the animals milling around and men studiously attempting to ignore her, yet casting sideways glances in her direction.

Trickles of sunlight filtered down from above. A stairway led up to a narrow walk that disappeared into the first level. She thought of the men standing up top in the clear breeze and sunlight and how lucky they were compared to those trapped inside the stone walls in the dim light. The air here stunk of animal droppings and the sweat of men. A goat approached her, favoring one hoof.

Though the goat didn't speak, she knew it was asking for help, that it knew what she was, that she was different from the men.

"Yes, I will help you," she said, kneeling in the straw-filled mud to examine the goat's foot. An angry red gash lay hidden just under the fur. It looked like perhaps one of the horses had stepped on it with their large, sharp hooves.

Not thinking about the filth she was reaching into, Amira sunk her hand into the mud rich with soil and water and insects, drawing the energy from them to heal the goat.

When she looked at the foot again, the wound was healed over. Only a scar remained under the grey-brown fur.

"There, you go. All better now." She patted the goat on the head. It nuzzled against her hand and then trotted off.

When she stood, she realized a man was watching her. Actually watching, not hiding his gaze like the others.

It wasn't the red plumed guard. This one didn't wear armor, but fine clothes, like those the king had worn. He had no crown upon his head of dark curls that hung just past his ears. A thick dark beard covered his cheeks and chin. With all the hair, she couldn't tell if he was smiling or not.

What had the guard called him? "Prince Gerald?" she asked.

"Yes," he said, half coughing. He covered his mouth with one hand until he'd cleared his throat. "Do you have a name?"

"Amira."

His eyes widened. "Amira?" He stepped backward, his back coming up short against the stone wall. There wasn't much room to move.

She pondered the handsome young man before her.

"It is strange to see you grown. It seems only a season since you were a baby in my arms."

"That cannot be." He shook his head. "You are Spindelkin."

"Yes? I don't expect that you would remember. You'd just been born. When we parted you were only days old. Did your mother treat you well?"

He was still shaking his head. "I...have to go. We will talk later." The prince darted over to a servant dressed in drab brown clothes like her maids had always worn. They spoke for a few minutes and then the prince ran up the stairs and vanished into the upper levels of the tower.

19

REUNION

The servant approached her, doing his best not to look at her straight on. It was rather comical, she thought.

"I won't curse you. Just bring me where I am to rest. And fresh water would be appreciated."

"You speak well for a creature of the forest," he whispered.

"I did grow up in your castle. The queen wouldn't stand for me speaking otherwise."

He hurried her up the stairs, which led to a narrow walkway that became a platform with a door on one side and a ladder on the other. They took the ladder up two levels and then took the door there to one of the three rooms inside.

"You are to stay here. Prince Gerald will call on you when he wishes."

"Thank you, and the water?"

He nodded and bowed his head as he backed away. Then he seemed to realize what he was doing and who she was, and instead turned and darted out the door, closing it behind him.

The inside of the room was dark, lit only by a tiny slit in the stone. A cool breeze wafted in. Nothing was living to speak to, and there was very little light. The servant hadn't left a candle. Figuring the prince would be a while, Amira settled onto the narrow mattress and pulled the blanket over herself. It seemed like years since she'd felt a bed, a blanket, or a mattress. All things she'd never thought of as out of the ordinary until she'd been away from them. She missed the smell of the forest, of the animals that sometimes curled up beside her to sleep. Everything here felt cold and dead. A chill settled over her that the blanket couldn't drive away.

A knock at the door startled Amira awake.

"Yes?" she called out.

"The prince will see you now."

Amira slid off the bed and went to the door, keeping the blanket about her shoulders. The leaf dress had been comfortable in the forest, but here, it didn't keep her warm and the leaves had turned stiff and dry.

The servant who had brought her to the room now led her from it. "Are you ill?" he asked.

"It is cold here," she said, wishing she had a second blanket.

"No different than outside," he shrugged.

"Everything here is dead."

At that, the servant turned away and didn't look at her or speak to her again. He moved quickly as though he couldn't wait to get away. They went down to the first level, where he pushed open the door to a room. The window there had been covered and only a few candles lit the space. The prince stood inside. He wasn't smiling.

Amira took a step inside. The servant closed the door behind her. A rhythmic chant came from beside her. Two guards stood in the shadows. She recognized it as the prayer the servants had used in the castle when she'd escaped. She shivered and pulled the blanket tighter around her shoulders.

"Amira, will you have a seat?" Prince Gerald asked. He pointed to two chairs and took one himself.

What she wanted was to see the sun, to go back outside, but if he was willing to talk, she would like that too. She went to the chair and sat.

Guards rushed at her, slipping a sack over her head that prevented her from seeing if they were only harming her or the prince too.

"Prince Gerald, are you well?"

"Don't worry about me. The queen wishes to speak to you, Amira. You have many crimes to answer for."

"Crimes? I haven't done anything wrong."

Someone pulled her from the chair, but the footsteps around her paused. Someone was breathing hard and sweating. She could smell it. Something metal clanked as another set of footsteps approached.

"Give them to me then, if you're so scared," said the

prince.

Cold metal wound around her until she couldn't move her arms. The iron leeched the energy from her body. Within a minute, she couldn't stand. She fell to her knees on the dried old wood that had long ago lost its voice and true form.

"See there, she's harmless now. Just as the queen said she would be," said the prince. "Bring her down to the wagon. We'll take her to the castle at once."

"No, please. I only wish to talk to you," she begged.

One of the guards picked her up and tossed her over his shoulder. Her world turned upside down.

The prince leaned in close. "We have a special room for your kind in the dungeon. You'll never see the sun again."

Terror filled Amira. She couldn't go back to that room again, not now that she'd felt the sun and talked to the trees. Try as she might to work her way free, her muscles had no strength.

The guard tromped down the stairs, bouncing her against his wide shoulder with each step. When he reached the bottom, the smell of wet fur and animal dung penetrated the bag. A horse neighed, then another. Hooves pounded.

"Get those horses under control," yelled the prince.

The guard carrying her staggered to one side. A goat bleated.

"Stupid goat! I'll eat you for dinner!" the guard shouted.

His steps turned into a trot and then she was dropped onto a hard wooden surface.

"Go on, get her out of here before she causes more trouble," said the prince.

The wagon lurched forward. The gate hinges creaked. Then they were out in fresh air, the wheels of the wagon clunking over stones on the dirt road. The clomping of three other sets of hooves joined the cart horses.

They raced over the road. Each jarring rock made her bounce hard against the bed of the wagon, taking her breath away.

Amira struggled to roll over but found herself wedged between what felt like cloth sacks and a barrel. At least out here, under the open sky, sunlight touched her skin in the few places not covered by the bag on her head, the blanket the chains had pinned to her shoulders, or the remains of her crumbling leaf dress. Even though the sun did warm her a little, the chains sucked the energy away almost as fast as she gained it. She didn't want to think about how the queen had discovered the chain's power over a Spindelkin.

When the sunlight faded and the air grew cold, they slowed and finally came to a stop, but they kept the wagon on the open road, far from any trees. They even led the horses away from the wagon so she couldn't ask them to help her escape.

They'd spend three nights on the road before the sounds of the countryside changed. There were voices, an axe chopping wood, and a dog barking.

Someone shouted, "Prince Gerald has returned!"

Other voices cheered.

Eventually, the wagon came to a stop.

"Take her down to the dungeon, all of you. And keep those chains in place. See that she encounters no mishaps along the way. The Queen will be overjoyed to see this one at last."

Amira wanted to run and hide, to call to the horses and any other animals that might come to her aid, to cry out to the trees, but she could feel that they were already in the castle walls. The surrounding stone made everything too quiet.

All the time she'd lived in the castle she'd thought the hollow, empty feeling was normal, but now she knew better. Now it felt like a bright beautiful light and warmth had been sucked from her body, leaving her only a shell.

Someone pulled her from the wagon. The bouncing began again as they carried her inside. They must have entered at a different place in the castle than she'd left because they were on the stairs going downward far too quickly. The lighting was dim with occasional bright spots. She didn't need to see to know where they were taking her.

The sound of the familiar heavy wooden door opening filled her with dread. Calloused hands put her down on cold stone. The door closed. The lock clicked. Amira lay on the floor of the pitch-black room, bound in the heavy chains, and cried.

20

DARKNESS

Amira didn't know how much time had passed in the darkness before voices drifted through the door of her prison. The clanking of the key in the lock made her heart beat faster. She sat against the wall she'd managed to work her way over to in the long hours she'd been left alone.

The door opened.

"Are you sure this is the one?" asked a voice Amira had hoped to never hear again. The queen.

"Yes, mother. She said her name was Amira."

"Take off that hood then. Let's have a look."

Footsteps shuffled closer.

"She can't harm you while she's in chains. Go on," she said.

Prince Gerald pulled the bag from Amira's head. In the soft glow of the candle he held, Amira could see the hints of the child's face she fondly remembered. If only he did too.

"I named you Corvin. Do you remember?"

He went still.

"What did she say?" The queen, dressed in one of her fine gowns and adorned with sparkling jewels, came closer, bringing her own candle.

The queen brought her flame close to Amira's face, blinding her. "You've done well, Gerald. Your father would be proud."

"The king, is he well?" Amira asked. While she wanted to be far from the queen, she did want to see the king again. He'd tried to help her and he'd been kind.

The prince gave her an odd look and then glanced at the queen. Neither of them answered her question.

"All grown up now, are you?" She nudged Amira with her foot. "Did you run out of your kin to send after us?"

"I didn't send anyone. You started a war by stealing me from the Spindelskov," said Amira.

"I didn't steal anyone," said the queen indignantly. "You did this."

Amira looked up at the face she'd thought was beautiful when she was a child—before she'd learned what beauty truly was. "What did I do?"

"You drove my father mad," said the prince, suddenly right next to his mother and looking so very angry. "You cursed our land and sent your horde of monsters to kill us all. You turned our animals against us. Our people starved for years until your curse weakened and crops began to grow again. Now you'll pay for what you did."

The queen put a hand on Gerald's shoulder, pulling him away. "She will pay, don't you worry about that."

She took a key from within her dress and put it in the lock that Amira could now see in the chains around her.

"Is that safe?" asked the prince.

"She can't use her foul magic down here. Remember the other prisoners?"

"Yes, but she isn't wounded like they were," he said.

The queen gave Amira a jarring shake. "She will be if she doesn't behave."

Amira nodded. She was already plenty bruised and sore from the wagon ride and the heavy chains.

"See, she's smarter than the others were. You need to be wary around this one," the queen said as she unwound the chains.

The prince gathered up the fallen chain. "Yes, mother. What are we going to do with her?"

"She will live out her days here, undoing the curse she brought upon us."

"I haven't cursed anyone," Amira said. "You only want me here so you can steal my blood again."

With the chains gone, the hollowness subsided. Now that she knew what to look for, there was a little life here if she reached deep and far enough. It was enough to give her the strength to stand.

The queen gasped. "You dare accuse a queen of common theft?"

"Not common at all," Amira said.

The angrier Amira got, the farther she was able to reach to pull energy from the damp air and the dirt tracked in by the guard who had brought her there. A soft glow lit on her skin and her eyes grew stronger. Beyond the candlelight, she could see the room was empty of all the finery of her childhood prison. She could smell the faint scent of other Spindelkin who had been kept here. Kin who were here no longer.

"You stole me from the Spindelskov, from my people. You imprisoned me here in this very room. You took my blood every day for eleven years to try to bring life back to the land you ruined." Amira pointed to the prince. "You used my blood to create your son and then you left him to die."

"Lies!" The queen struck Amira on the cheek. "You wretched monster. Your kind will be driven from this land."

The prince flinched but did nothing to stop the queen.

"Leave her here for a few days and then we'll see if she's ready to confess."

21

QUESTIONS

Long hours passed as Amira sat on the cold stone floor, glad for at least the blanket she'd taken from the tower. A tickling on her foot caught her attention, tugging her from her dismal thoughts. Though she couldn't see what it was, memories from her stay in this room before supplied the cause. A spider.

She resisted the urge to swat it away and instead tried to talk to it. "Well met, spider. Are you trapped here too?"

Minutes slipped by but the spider didn't answer. However, it did stop moving. It was so still, that she began to wonder if she'd imagined it was there at all. Then she felt the tiny tickles of another set of legs, and then another.

"Are you lonely too?" she asked. "I suppose I can't be picky about my company, can I?"

The spiders didn't respond, but they did settle in.

Spiders would not have been her choice of companion. Neither would mice, though they were cheerful enough and did enjoy being petted now and then. Spiders, well, they didn't keep her warm and it wasn't like she could pet them, and they didn't talk, but at least she knew she wasn't alone.

Amira tried to sleep as much as she could to conserve what energy she had. When she woke the first time, the spiders were gone, or at least off of her skin, but a mouse had curled up on her lap. She stroked its soft fur. It squeaked and made a chirping noise, but didn't talk and she couldn't understand its mouse noises. When she woke the next time it was to the sound of the door opening.

In the faint light from the hallway, she could see it was only one person and they didn't bring a candle inside. From the shape, it didn't appear to be the queen. That was a small relief.

"I'll be right outside if you need me, your highness," said someone outside the room.

"Amira?"

"Prince Gerald?" While she was relieved it wasn't the queen, the prince hadn't been at all kind to her either. She pressed herself against the wall for the lack of anywhere to hide, though they were both in total darkness.

"I have a dagger so think twice before you do anything foolish," he said.

"What is it that you think I will do?" she asked.

"Your kind is full of evil tricks. My mother witnessed many foul things when you sent your minions from the Spindelskov to attack us."

"They did set out to attack you, but I didn't send them. I was only a child, and I'd never met my people before that. Does it make sense that they would listen to me, a stranger and a child?"

"I don't know," he said uncertainly. "I came here to ask you about something you said earlier."

"Does the queen know that you are here?"

He was quiet a moment, feet shuffling on the stone. "She thinks I'm out hunting. And I will be after you tell me what you meant about her using your blood and leaving me to die."

"I so wanted a brother or sister," she said, remembering her excitement. "The queen was my mother, or so I thought. She raised me here, in this room, though it was filled with fine things then. And light. Do you have a candle?"

"You're talking nonsense. Mother said you can't be trusted." His footsteps moved toward the door.

"Wait. The queen lost many babies before you. She'd been taking blood from me for years, though she told me it was poison and that she was trying to help me. I'm not sure what she did with it all, but from what your father hinted at the last time we spoke, she may have swallowed a drop or two to help keep you strong in her belly."

He snorted. "That's ridiculous. Everyone knows

that Spindelkin blood is deadly."

"Did they ever free all the maids who had served me? The ones she locked away?"

His footsteps came closer again. "There were no maids in the other cells, only monsters like you. Ill-formed creatures who wailed day and night."

Tears rolled down Amira's cheeks. "They were innocent. Those poor women."

"What do you mean?" Fabric rustled and leather creaked as the prince sat on the stone nearby.

"During my treatments, sometimes a drop of blood would spill and they would touch it by accident, or foolishly try to clean it up. They would go still. I thought they died, but now I think they must have started to change. Some of the maids, your mother just didn't like, maybe they asked too many questions, but she would scream at them and I'd never see them again. When I snuck out of this room, the day you were born, I heard the wailing. I didn't know what it was. Jancy, a kind woman your father sent to help me, hurried me through the dungeon to get to you."

"If she used your blood to keep me, why am I not a monster too?" he asked quietly.

Amira drew a deep breath, not appreciating being called a monster and hoping the truth wouldn't send him running out the door. "You were born much like me. A beautiful child, but not what your mother wanted. The king was so angry with her that he left the castle. She deserted you in the room where you were born, cold and hungry. She did not name you or claim you. I found you there, crying."

"That can't be true. I look like my father and nothing like you."

"Because I took you out into the courtyard with the fountain full of tiny fish and mossy rocks beneath my bare feet. I felt sunshine for the first time there with you in my arms." She smiled, thinking of how wondrous the sun had been when she first saw it.

"You've been in the queen's courtyard?"

"If that's what you call it. I fed you in the way of our kind."

He gasped. "You fed me the flesh of men?"

Amira laughed. "Is that what your mother tells people?"

"Your teeth can tear the flesh from men in minutes."

"Foolish lies. The sun feeds us just like the trees and plants. The only time I ate flesh was when your mother fed it to me, and it was pig, deer, or birds. Your food kept me alive, but it wasn't what my body needed. She kept me from the sun so that I would stay small and weak."

"But then why am I not a monster?"

"I wanted you to live so I tried to make you better. I'd never had enough strength to do anything like that before, but when I pushed energy into you, it pushed out the parts that were kin. The queen was very happy that you weren't like me anymore."

"She said you cursed me, that you were the one who gave me—"

"The golden scales on your cheek?" she guessed.

He jumped to his feet and ran for the door. At first, she thought he had left, but then she heard him speaking to someone. He returned with a candle.

The prince again sat on the floor in front of her, but now the candle sat between them, casting a soft glow over his stunned face.

"How do you know about those?" he asked.

"You were covered in beautiful, shimmering fine scales. I kissed your cheek as I pushed energy into your tiny, frail body. When I pulled away, the only hint of kin left was where my lips had been."

He touched his beard where the scales lay underneath. "That's not how my mother tells the story."

Amira smiled. "I bet not. She told me stories too. All lies."

He shook his head. "She said that you stole me from her, that you took me away to offer me to the trees of Spindelskov to spite her."

"That's what I told her." Amira leaned in toward the scant warmth of the single flame. "I was very angry that she'd left you to die and then suddenly loved you once you were like her. It was then that I realized she wasn't my mother. That your father who had been kind to me was not my father."

He bit his lower lip and watched the flame between them. "You knew my father?"

She nodded. "He would come to play with me and read me stories. He was very sad the last time I saw him.

I was very sick then."

The prince picked at the stitching on his coat. "He stays at the country estate. I used to go there for part of the year to live with him. He has little love for the queen."

"Why did you say he was crazy?"

The prince watched her intently. "He was always going on about a daughter he lost. My mother was adamant that she never had a daughter. She said he was crazy and so did everyone else."

Amira smiled sadly. He had missed her. She missed him too. "Do you think I might see him?"

"You would want to? He's one of us."

Amira pondered that for a moment. "For eleven years, I was told I was one of you. I didn't know any different until I saw how your mother looked at you once you were like her. Then all the pieces fell together. Other than the queen, I've never had hard feelings for any of you."

His eyes grew wide. "But the curse! And the war. And—"

"There was never a curse." Amira shook her head. "Your mother used my blood to make things grow, like in the field where my people fell."

"But the grass, the plants, the flowers, everything is so lush there. And here, our harvests are weak. Nothing grows well. Our animals are thin, but no one dares hunt near the Spindelskov where the game animals are healthy."

Amira thought about what the elders had shared

with her on the ride back to Gorsia. "Your people drove us out. They cut down the trees. It was your people that cursed this land, not us."

He sat there, picking at his fingers, avoiding her gaze. The flame flickered. The silence drew out. A mouse, maybe the same one, crept out of the shadows along the wall to slip up into Amira's lap.

The prince scowled at the mouse. "The vermin down here are impossible to manage. Get that thing off of you."

"It's fine. It just wants to be warm, no different than me." She stroked its back. "None of the animals talk here. Do you know why?"

He gave her a strange look. "Animals don't talk. They make noises."

"You understood them once. I'm sorry I took that from you."

"I'm glad you did. That would be very strange. I don't think I would like it."

She almost didn't want to know the answer, but curiosity made her ask, "Did your mother treat you well?"

"Yes, she did. I think. I guess I wouldn't know any better."

"You would."

He smiled. She realized it was the first time she'd seen him do that.

"You look like your father when you smile," she said.

"Why did you call me Corvin? My mother has never used that name, but when you said it, it felt right, but no one else has ever called me that. So how did I know it?"

"It was the name of a boy in a story that your father often read to me. The queen didn't name you, and when I took you with me to the Spindelskov, I couldn't very well keep calling you baby."

"But why did you take me with you if it wasn't to offer me up to the trees?"

"Firstly, the trees of Spindelskov don't eat babies. Or anything else but what the sun, rain, and soil offer." She winked at him. "But mostly it was because I was furious with all of her lies and then having no care for her own son just because he was different than her. Because he was more like me."

"So what did you plan to do with me? You say you were a child yourself."

"All I knew was that I didn't want you to be here with that horrible woman who didn't love you. I'd never met my kind. I didn't know what to expect. I guess maybe I didn't want to be alone either."

Amira sat against the wall, not nearly as cold as she had been, if even for only the company. She told him of their adventures of traveling to the Spindelskov with the help of the animals. He laughed when she told him about his cries ruining her first sun ceremony and then he seemed to realize she wasn't laughing.

"I'm sorry? I guess? I was an infant. What did you expect?"

She did smile then. "I knew nothing of infants. I still don't. My people grow differently."

Amira told him of the time differences in the forest.

"Wait, so for you, it has only been a year or two?"

She shrugged. "It's hard to tell, but not near long enough for you to be fully grown."

"When we captured you in the tower, you asked after me. Why?"

"I didn't know if the guards were attacking you too."

He rose to his knees, stretching. "It seems my mother has lied about many things."

"Are you leaving then?" The thought of being alone in the dark again filled her with sadness.

"I must. I'm supposed to be hunting. If I don't come back with something, she'll ask questions." He stood and looked down at her. "I'm sorry that I have to take the candle. Can I bring you anything?"

"You'll come back then?"

"When I can. Do you need food or water? I'm afraid I can't manage much else without my mother finding out."

"Water would be welcome. Sunlight would be wonderful."

"Sorry about the chains." He stared at the floor. "And everything else. I didn't know."

While she was grateful that he'd listened to her and seemed sorry, she wasn't ready to forgive him just yet.

"Don't forget your candle."

He reached down to pick it up, keeping an eye on her the whole time. Then he backed away to the door. It seemed he wasn't quite ready to trust her either.

22

TRUTHS

When the door opened next it was a woman's voice. One she had no desire to hear, one that made her cringe in the darkness and huddle against the cold, stone wall. Though she knew she couldn't hide, she pulled the blanket tight around herself anyway.

The queen carried a lantern that offered more light than the bare candle Prince Gerald had brought. Her skirts rustled over the stone. She regarded Amira with downturned lips. "Pathetic little creature. You're lucky we need you. The others were too wounded to do much good before they died."

"Where did they die?" Amira asked, wondering if there might be trees wallowing down here in the dungeon somewhere.

"In this very room. They faded into nothing more than dust. At least your kind are tidy when they pass from living to dead. No troublesome bodies to dispose of. Gerald, quit dawdling. It's time you learn how to save the kingdom that will one day be yours."

A second lantern brightened the room. The man carrying it did not look at all happy. He avoided Amira's gaze.

"Now then, hand me the knife so we can get started." The queen held out her hand.

It was then that Amira noticed the bundle that the prince carried under his other arm. He knelt and spread out the cloth to reveal a familiar bottle, but this time there was no tube or needle. Just the bottle and a knife and a jug of water.

The prince handed the knife to the queen but continued in front of her to hand the jug to Amira. "Can't have you drying out," he said.

His fingers lingered when she took the jug, and for a moment, his gaze was filled with an apology, but then it vanished.

"Good, let's get started," the queen announced.

The queen set the bottle on the floor by her feet and grabbed Amira's hand. She sliced Amira's finger with the knife. Golden blood welled in the cut. Before the queen could guide Amira's finger over the bottle, Amira jerked her hand back, sprinkling her blood on the wall and floor.

The queen snarled. "Selfish creature! You curse our land and then waste the cure."

"My blood is mine to waste. You took enough from me for something I never did. The curse upon this land is your own."

Amira sucked on her cut finger, then wrapped it with a corner of her blanket.

The queen raised the knife again, reaching for Amira with her other hand. The prince grabbed his mother's arm.

"Stop," he said. "Look."

Amira glanced around her to find lilies sprouting from the stone just as they had once before. Leaves had sprung from the wall behind her, and on the floor around her. The plants grew so much faster than she remembered from the first time, but she was older now, healthier.

The queen jerked her arm back. "How dare you touch me?"

"She was telling the truth," said the prince. "Those are the same flowers that are in the field where you say the war with the Spindelkin happened. He stood between her and Amira. "Did you keep Amira here in this room before?"

The queen stood up straight and kept the knife in her hand, eyeing Amira. "This is the room we keep Spindelkin prisoners, yes."

"Answer the question, Mother."

"Amira was a prisoner here before you were born," she said.

"And was I like her when I was born?"

Her mouth dropped open. "Who told you such a thing? What a terrible rumor. I will have their tongue."

Prince Gerald looked to Amira. She nodded.

"I think, Mother, that your time as queen has come to an end." He squeezed her arm until the knife clattered to the floor.

"Amira, go to the door. Take a lantern with you," he instructed.

Not waiting for him to change his mind, Amira did as Prince Gerald asked. She stood by the door and waited while the prince spoke quietly to the queen. He backed her against the wall where Amira had sat and pushed her arm until she crouched down. Her skirts puddled around her as though she were a flower bursting from a massive bud. Amira couldn't see her face with the prince in the way, but she knew the tone well. The queen was livid.

Prince Gerald let her go and then grabbed the knife and the other lantern. "I'll send someone with a meal later, Mother. Enjoy the flowers."

The prince backed away, holding the lantern out so he could see where she still huddled on the floor.

He reached back to pull the door open and nudged Amira out of the room.

"Could you cover your head with your blanket? Just this once. Until we get this sorted out?"

Amira remembered how much easier it was to get through the castle with the cloak and hood covering her face. "Yes, I can do that."

Using the blanket like a cloak, she bunched up one end to cover her head like a hood and draped the rest over her shoulders.

"Follow me."

While Amira sort of remembered the way through the dungeon, she knew she'd be very lost if he allowed her up into the castle. The one improvement over the last trip through the dungeon was that there was no moaning or screaming. In fact, it was mostly silent.

"The dungeon is empty?" she whispered, afraid to break the quiet.

"No. Mother was sick of the noise."

Amira recalled what the queen had said about taking her tongue and grimaced. She crept closer to the prince.

"Don't worry, I won't let her harm you again," he said. "Hurry, I need to find a safe place for you while I explain what's going on to the guards. Most of them will follow me, but I don't know about all of them."

She couldn't argue with that plan. "Do you have somewhere with a window? I would appreciate it. I miss the sun."

"It's a cloudy day, I'm afraid, but yes, I think I can manage that."

"Thank you."

He turned around and grinned. "I think I know just the place."

Before she could argue, he took her hand and rushed through the dungeon. She had to run to keep up with his much longer legs.

In the back of her mind, she didn't know if this

perfect place was a different cell in the dungeon or a room in the castle, but he was intent on getting there in a hurry. When they came to the stairway with a guard at the bottom, her breath caught in her throat.

"You're really going to let me go up there?"

"I said I was, didn't I?"

She quite liked the way the lantern light twinkled in his eyes. Amira nodded.

"Well then, let's go." He guided her over to the guard.

"Who is this then?"

"A guest. She will be joining me for dinner."

"And the queen? She is not with you?"

Prince Gerald drew himself up tall. "The queen will be staying here awhile."

"In the dungeon? Is she with that monster?"

"No. She has her own crimes to answer for."

"I don't know as we can do that, your highness."

"You're going to. I will explain tonight. At least give me until then."

The guard cringed. "She'll have my head."

"I'll see that she doesn't." The prince started up one stair and then paused. "As a matter of fact, how about you be busy elsewhere? Could you get a message to the king?"

"I suppose I could do that."

"Tell him Amira is at the castle."

"Who's Amira?" asked the guard.

"He'll know what it means."

Grateful the prince was going to give her the chance

to speak to the king, Amira squeezed his hand. "Thank you."

"Let's see how this all goes before you thank me."

She nodded.

He took the stairs two at a time, forcing her to jump from one to the next, before coming to a sudden halt. "I'm sorry, I'm not used to someone so little."

"I'm much bigger than I was, I'll have you know," she said between breaths.

"It's not a bad size. I'm just not used to it," he said softly.

Mollified, Amira hurried up the stairs with him until they came to the top door. Another guard stood there.

"Your highness." He bowed.

"The Queen will be awhile."

"Very well." He swung the door open.

They headed in a familiar direction.

"Why are we going toward the queen's rooms?" she asked.

"You remember your way around?"

"As I said, it wasn't that long ago for me."

He shrugged. "If the queen is busy elsewhere, no one will be in her rooms. Her maids will be attending to other duties before dinner."

They hurried down the same halls she'd traveled with Jancy. But with the prince at her side, no one stopped them. No one even questioned them. The guards and servants all bowed and went about their business.

They made quick time to a door that the prince pushed open.

Amira stopped in the doorway. "Not this room."

"Why? What's wrong with it?"

Everything inside had changed, but her heart knew exactly what this room was. The barren furnishings had been replaced with luxurious ones. The bed was piled high with furs and pillows. It stood so tall that it had a step, just like hers used to.

"This is the room where you were born. The room where I found you. Where she left you."

"She's lived in this room since I can remember."

"Would you mind if I stayed in the courtyard instead?"

"It's cold. It might rain."

"I don't mind."

He glanced around the room and then darted for a chest. The prince pulled it open and rifled through the contents. "She kept an old cloak in here when I was younger, when she'd take me out into the courtyard to play."

The prince grinned when he came out with a green cloak in his hand. "Here it is. Whatever happens, you can keep this one. I'm sure she won't miss it. I haven't seen her wear it in years."

Amira pulled the blanket from her head and shoulders and stood shivering in the big room. The leaves of her dress crumbled away at her touch. She'd have to do something about that soon or borrow more from the queen's wardrobe.

Prince Gerald settled the long green cloak about her shoulders and tied the string that held it closed at her neck.

"Better?"

She nodded. "I'm sorry, I'm rather a mess right now. The queen would have had a fit to see me like this when I was a child."

"She is quite bothered with appearances, isn't she?" The prince chuckled. "I don't mind. You look like a wild, forest sprite."

Was he teasing her? "Sprites are only a creature of your storybooks, you know."

He held up his hand. "I did not, but now I do."

Deciding he was only having fun, she smiled. "Be careful out there. While I am grateful for the queen's current lodgings, I'm not sure that the rest of the court will be."

"Thank you for showing me the truth, Amira."

With that, Prince Gerald led her to the door that went out into the courtyard. "Make sure you stay here and out of sight. I'll come back for you as soon as I can."

23

THE COURTYARD

Amira tucked herself back into a corner of the courtyard between the tree where the birds that had carried her away had been long ago and a shrub with bright yellow leaves. It was autumn here, she realized. The seasons didn't change much in the Spindelskov, but outside, the world did, just as time moved differently here. She watched the clouds overhead in the grey sky, wondering how much time was passing in the forest. How large would the elders' trees be when she returned? If she returned, she amended. The prince seemed nice enough now, but his mother had raised him. And her court might be more loyal to her than he thought.

Birds flitted overhead, landing in the tree and on the stone, pecking at fallen bits on the ground. The fountain burbled in the center. Though she wanted to go over and see if fish still swam in the water, she liked her hiding spot and was hesitant to leave it.

The prince had mentioned dinner. Something would need to be done about her dress. Now that she was back outside, she could feel her strength returning even though the sun was behind thick clouds. Just breathing fresh air and being surrounded by the few plants in the courtyard helped.

Amira considered the dress she'd thought to create when she had first set out to enter Katra. A grand gown that rivaled the queen's would be fitting for a dinner with the prince. And if by chance, she was destined to return to the dungeon, she could at least do so in a fresh, clean dress.

She surveyed her nearby options. While she thought she could maybe summon leaves from beyond the castle walls, that would certainly attract attention. It would be better to take from the courtyard where no one would notice.

The one large tree held fiery red leaves edged with orange. Those would do nicely. Pressing her hand to the trunk of the tree, she opened her mind to it, finding the voice deep inside the wood. It was old and faint. The tree let out a long exhale.

"It has been so long since I've heard a voice such as yours."

"The people here have kept us away. I am sorry, dear tree. Is there anything I can do for you in return for your leaves?"

"These stones are too tight. They keep the rain from reaching my roots. They are choking me."

Amira sank to her knees and called to the soil. She asked it to push up and loosen the stones. One by one, the stones near the trunk of the tree popped out of the ground, scraping over the ones nearby. She stepped around the tree, choosing a stone here and there to pop out with the help of the soil. With an assortment of stones loosened, she pushed them aside. Then she darted over to the fountain to gather up a handful of moss.

Depositing a tiny bit of the moss in each opening, she distributed her handful and helped the moss flourish until it filled the spaces. Now, her work looked like it had been there all along. Except for all the loose stones. With a heavy sigh, Amira set about piling up all the extra stones against the wall. It might not look natural, she considered, admiring her handiwork, but at least she had a spot to sit while she waited for the prince to hopefully come back.

"Thank you," said the tree.

Amira hugged the trunk. "I'm sorry you have gone so long without any help here."

The tree filled her with appreciation. "Take my leaves. I am done with them for the season. It pleases me that they will go to good use instead of being carted off by a man."

After making sure all the windows facing the courtyard were empty, she released the shape of her dress. The remains of the leaves fell with a swoosh onto the stones at her feet and gently blew away.

She hung the cloak on a branch and summoned

new leaves to her in a far more intricate pattern than she'd ever attempted before. After forming the base for the dress, she also reached out to a bush, summoning some of the yellow leaves for the front of the bodice.

Feeling warm at last and refreshed, Amira admired her work. The red leaves formed a wide skirt that wisped over the stones as she turned one way and then the other to test the flow of the leaves. They all performed perfectly, the many layers holding their massive form effortlessly. Smaller yellow leaves ran up her chest, surrounded by the red, leaving her neck and arms bare. While she didn't have any of the queen's jewels and her hair was still a frightful mess from the ride with the bag over her head, she felt a hundred times better and almost as though she belonged in the castle.

Amira started when a bird landed on her head. And then two more joined it. The blue feathered birds twittered as they hopped around, their beaks busily darting in and out of the tangled mess of her hair.

A swirl of wind kicked up a handful of shiny ivory seed hulls, sweeping them into a pile. A large spider, like the one she'd felt down in the dungeon, hurried over to them and began spinning a web.

A line of black beetles paraded from the bush in the far corner, each bearing a red berry in their pincers. They deposited the berries next to the spider. The birds tittered as they worked and finally came to a stop on her shoulder. Amira patted each of them on their little feathered heads and thanked them for their help, even if they couldn't talk back. They chittered happily and flew up to perch in the now bare tree branches.

Finished with its work, the spider scuttled over, dragging its creation along with it. Its long legs made quick work of climbing up her dress and onto her shoulders to come around behind her neck. Its fuzzy feet tickled. She tried not to move while it fastened the necklace in place. The intricate creation fit perfectly, a piece that even the queen would be jealous of. Or maybe not, since it didn't contain any real jewels. As far as Amira was concerned, this felt far better on her skin than any of the fancy gowns she'd worn as a child.

Four mice skittered over to deliver tiny white flowers from the vines crawling up the courtyard wall. They deposited the blooms in her hair, tucking them in with their tiny toes.

Her feet were bare but she didn't want it any other way. She loved the feel of the soil and stone. It felt right, energy flowing up from the ground into her skin.

Amira sent out her thanks to all the creatures and plants in the courtyard.

She pulled the cloak back over her shoulders and carefully pulled the hood over her head. A light sprinkle began to fall. Amira sat on the stack of stones. The bush blocked most of the drizzle and the cloak kept her dry.

The light had mostly dimmed from the sky before the door to the courtyard opened. Amira held her breath, waiting to see who would emerge from the castle.

Her heart sunk when it wasn't the prince. Though

she wasn't sure what exactly to make of him yet, he was a welcome face. And a handsome one at that. Being near him felt familiar, perhaps because he still harbored a bit of Spindelkin within him, or maybe it was the connection she'd forged between them when she'd fed him from the earth as an infant. She looked forward to finding out more about him.

A servant peered around the courtyard. Finally, she called out, "Mistress Amira? Are you here?"

Not knowing if she should trust the woman or not, she stayed in the deep shadows of the corner.

"I'm here. Where is Prince Gerald?"

"He has asked me to bring you to him. He's in the hall. Dinner is about to be served."

If she was telling the truth, that was very promising indeed, but if the queen had twisted him back to her will, Amira might find herself back in the dungeon. She remained on her bench.

"He asked me to give you this as a token of good faith." The servant held up the knife the prince had taken from the queen.

If he was offering her a weapon, she did feel better about trusting the servant. Amira gathered up her skirt and emerged from behind the shrub.

"Leave it on the ground and back away."

The servant did as she asked.

Amira hurried as much as her new gown allowed and picked up the knife. No one rushed out of the shadows to grab her. The servant simply held the door.

"This way, mistress."

Again covered with a cloak, Amira wasn't stopped on her way to the hall. The servant bustled right along, not giving her a second glance. Amira began to wonder if Prince Gerald had told anyone who she was. Or that the queen was in the dungeon, or why.

They came to the open doors of the great hall. The room was filled with people dressed in their finest, lining the tables laden with food. Thank the trees she'd managed a change into an appropriate dress. Amira slipped the knife into the pocket inside the cloak. It wouldn't do to be seen approaching the prince with a weapon in hand, even if the tables were lined with people with similar knives for cutting their food. The rules were different for her.

The servant stayed at the doors. "Go on. He's asked you to join him at the head table. There's an empty seat for you there."

Amira took one step into the room. Heads swiveled to her. It was hard to see the full reaction with the hood in place, but she didn't dare remove it, not until the prince said it was safe.

If it was safe at all.

24

DINNER

With each step Amira took into the room, it seemed like more people noticed her, more people stopped moving, stopped speaking. Her nerves sang.

The prince noticed her too. He stood and announced, "Our guest has arrived."

All conversation ended abruptly. Amira froze. Instinct told her to run for the doors, to keep running until she was out of the castle. But if the prince was going to make an effort to bring an understanding to Katra, her running out the door would ruin that in an instant. If she could be brave and withstand the stares and hope his intentions were honest, she might end the enmity between Katra and the Spindelkin. She could bring peace to her people and Prince Gerald to his.

The prince beckoned her closer to the table where he stood. A spot was indeed open next to him. But that made sense, she considered. That was likely where the queen was to sit. Not her. But when she glanced over the rest of the table, there were no other empty seats. She couldn't take the queen's chair. The queen would never forgive that slight.

Her feet again halted and the urge to run for the door was stronger than ever. Her hands clutched the cloak at her sides. The knife was safe next to her right hand, but there were too many people. She wouldn't know where to start if it came to defending herself.

"Amira, would you join me?" asked the prince, holding out his hand to the empty chair beside him.

She took one halting step closer.

He gestured for her to remove her cloak. If she did so, there would be no turning back. She'd never make it out the door. Everyone would know what she was. Candlelight danced on all the knives on the tables and in the hands of the staring people.

She took a deep breath and let it out and then another. Her nerves refused to settle. Amira thought of the tree in the courtyard who hadn't heard the voice of her kind in generations. How many other plants here, the animals, the very soil itself, longed for the return of her kind? She owed it to them to try.

Amira carefully pulled back her hood. A collective gasp swept through the room. Bolstered by the fact no one surged forward to wrap chains around her, she slid the cloak from her shoulders and draped it over one arm, keeping the knife still relatively in reach.

One of the ladies at the head table screamed. Several of the men muttered prayers. Well over half of the room's occupants averted their eyes. The others couldn't seem to stop staring. Neither could Prince Gerald. He opened and closed his mouth several times but no words came out.

While everyone was occupied and no one appeared to be barring her way, Amira made her way around to the backside of the table to take the seat next to the prince.

"You changed," he said quietly.

"Is that a problem?" she asked, keeping her gaze on the crowd. More of whom were praying and looking at anything other than her.

"You look beautiful. Truly," he whispered.

A flood of warmth rushed through Amira as a smile swept over her lips.

He cleared his throat and stood up tall, addressing everyone in the hall with a clear voice. "Yes, Amira is of the Spindelkin. She is my guest. You will treat her as such."

"Where is the queen?" demanded one of the richly dressed men at their table who was now also on his feet.

Several more rose also, banging their fists on the table.

The prince held up his hands. "Let us explain. You all know the new spread of trees between the Spindelskov and the lookout tower."

"The monsters that dwell there are trying to get closer. If we don't cut them down, they'll overrun us in a generation or two," said one of the other men at their table. "Read your history."

"I have. Perhaps you didn't go back far enough. I sought out the old texts my father kept, the history our foolish ancestors tried to hide. There are maps that show that the trees covered all of Katra. Not as thick as the Spindelskov, but like in the spread. Our ancestors felled them to make their homes and plant their fields. What they didn't understand was that those trees were alive."

Chuckles erupted from the hall "Of course trees are alive."

The prince scowled. "Not alive that way. But actually alive as you and I are. The Spindelkin care for them and all of the land and animals."

He turned to Amira. "Is this not so?"

She tried to make her voice carry as well as his did, but she'd never addressed an audience like this. Certainly not one staring at her with malice and fear. "That is the truth."

"And when we cleared the land and hunted the kin, our land suffered."

"That's the curse of the kin!" yelled someone from the lower tables.

The prince shook his head. "No, that's a curse we brought on ourselves. My mother, your queen sought to avert this curse. She has secretly kept Spindelkin in the dungeon, draining them of their blood."

"Lies!" Chants of similar sentiments rose from the occupants of the hall.

"How dare you speak of the queen in such an ill way?" sputtered one of the well-dressed men at the end of their table.

"Do you recall the streak of prosperity Katra enjoyed in the years before my birth and again after the kin were slain by our iron?"

Heads nodded.

"That good luck was bought with Spindelkin blood. Your queen added their blood into the water used to irrigate the fields and the ponds where our animals drank. Diluted, it didn't cause much notice."

It occurred to Amira that this was perhaps how the queen had been able to take her blood to help remain pregnant without manifesting signs of the kin in herself.

"You have seen the field where the tree spread grows and the lilies that grow there?"

"Those are my favorite flowers," said one of the women nearby.

"Those flowers are born from the pure blood of the Spindelkin."

One of the men scoffed, "Blood doesn't grow flowers."

"Amira will prove that it does." He turned to her.

So that was why he'd offered her the knife. She didn't appreciate being put on display, but she supposed evidence was the easiest way to make them all believe. It had worked on Prince Gerald, after all.

But he didn't ask her to take out her knife. He motioned to the man sitting beside him, the one who kept mocking him, to stand and come over to Amira.

The prince held out a clean dagger from his belt to the man. "Poke gently. Do not seek to cause pain or you will receive the same."

Amira held out her hand for all to see and kept it visible while the man, now with a shaking hand under so much attention, took the dagger and pressed the tip to Amira's finger. A single drop welled there. She turned her hand over, letting the drop swell and drip onto an empty space on the table.

The room went silent as all the gazes were glued to the table. Those in the back stood, peering over the heads of the rest.

Nothing happened for several moments and then between one blink and the next, a seedling appeared.

It grew with amazing speed, leaves unfurling, stalk extending, bud forming, and within moments, a fully formed and blooming lily plant had grown from the table top. Gasps and murmurs drifted around the hall.

The woman who had remarked about the flowers stood and came over to smell the bloom. "That's the same flower!" she exclaimed.

The outspoken man returned the dagger to the prince and sat. He didn't say a word.

A bedraggled man ran through the doors of the hall and slid to a stop. He wore no crown upon his head and his beard had grown wild, hanging down to his waist and streaked with grey, but Amira knew him instantly and her heart swelled.

The king cautiously approached the head table. He wore a fur-lined cloak but it was worse for wear and his boots had holes in the toes. His hair hung long past his ears, looking much like he'd taken a knife to it himself.

"Amira?" he whispered.

Unable to help herself, Amira gathered up her skirt and rushed around the table to throw her arms around him. Her head didn't even reach his shoulders, but she hugged him all the same. His heartbeat against her ear brought back fond memories of playing games and listening to stories while sitting beside the younger version of this man.

"I'm glad you are well," she said.

His voice was thick and tears welled in his eyes. "Look at you. All grown up and beautiful."

"Thanks to you."

He smiled, patting her back. "You're going to make this grown man cry in front of the entire hall," he whispered.

"Is that so bad?" she asked, wiping a tear from her cheek.

"No, I suppose not." He squeezed her tightly. "They already think I'm crazy."

"But you are not."

"Where is the queen?" he asked, peering over her at the head table.

She stepped back, giving him space. "I think it would be wise to speak to your son about that. This was his doing, not mine."

"Worked your way into another man's heart, did you?" He chuckled.

"I hardly think so, we only just met." Yet, she felt a blush upon her cheeks that only grew warmer when she met Prince Gerald's gaze.

"Only just, huh?" The king shook his head, laughing.

25

Don't Make Her Angry

Prince Gerald approached Amira and the king, a wide smile upon his face. "It is good to see you, Father."

"And you." He embraced his son and clapped him on the back. "Thank you for the message."

"I'm sorry I sided with mother on keeping you away. I didn't know Amira was real. Not like this anyway, only that the Spindelkin were a threat to us."

"About your mother—"

"Sit, join us. We'll talk after we eat. You look like you could use a good meal."

They made their way back to the table. The outspoken man who had sat next to the prince, vacated his seat to offer it to the king.

"The queen does keep my allowance quite tight, I will admit."

"That will no longer be an issue," the prince stated

firmly.

The king's plate was quickly filled as was Amira's. The hall was abuzz with conversation, both hushed with pointing and the other half boisterous with celebration at the king's return. The king ate with great appetite. Amira picked at her food, nibbling here and there to be polite, but it wasn't the type of sustenance she needed.

"There was a maid who you sent to me, Jancy, do you know if she escaped the queen's wrath? I hate to think that she might still be in the dungeon," Amira asked the king.

He smiled. "Jancy did return to me at my estate. She's safe there. Happy. Has a few children of her own now."

Relieved, Amira tried a bite, but though the food looked wonderful, it had little taste. She wondered if any of her other maids were still in the dungeon and if she could convince Prince Gerald to free them.

A musician began to play, filling the hall with sweet sounds. Throughout the meal, the lily on the table in front of the king drew a lot of attention. Amira tried to ignore the pointing in her direction, to not glare at those leering at her, but it was difficult. Prince Gerald carried on a lively conversation with his father and the other noble families at their table. He tried to get her to join the conversation, but she was not familiar with most of what they were talking about. She began to long for the quiet of the forest.

"Amira," the prince said quietly, placing his hand

lightly atop hers where it rested on the table. "Are you unwell?"

"There are too many voices here. So many people. I..."

"I'm sorry, I should have considered that." He looked at her barely touched plate. "And I didn't think about the food. Forgive me, I will have to do better to remember our differences."

His hand was warm atop hers, pleasantly so. The open concern on his face made her heart flutter. "Not so terribly different, but thank you."

A great commotion erupted outside the hall. The shrieking voice of the furious queen rose above it all. Amira went still.

The prince swore under his breath.

The king gave him a strange look. "What's going on?"

"It seems my mother has escaped from the dungeon."

The queen stormed into the hall, her hair in disarray and her gown crumpled. The music came to an end, leaving the last note hanging in the sudden silence. The occupants of the hall craned around to see their queen.

"How dare you!" The queen pointed at Prince Gerald. "And then you have the nerve to put that monster in my place?" She bared her teeth in a ferocious snarl and rushed to the head table.

The king stood and hurried to Amira's side. "Let's let Gerald handle her. She likes him. Or did, anyway."

Amira wasn't about to argue, and she didn't know where to go on her own. She took the king's offered arm and hurried through the narrow door at the back of the hall, just behind the head table. On the other side of the door, they rushed down a long, narrow hallway. It ended in a door that opened to a familiar part of the castle, the doors to the courtyard and the queen's room were just ahead of them.

"I think it would be best if we left the castle until morning. My carriage is outside," said the king.

Outside sounded wonderful, anywhere that was away from so many people.

Instead of going to the left toward the courtyard, he turned right toward the central part of the castle. Amira regretted leaving her cloak in the hall. Everyone they met stared at her and muttered prayers, averting their eyes. Everyone, except the four guards standing between them and the door leading to the awaiting carriage.

"Halt, in the name of the queen!" shouted the guards.

The king stopped his forward march, pulling Amira up short beside him. "I'm sorry, Amira. I don't even have a sword on me. Not that I could defeat four guards in any case. My fighting days are long gone."

Amira took stock of the strength she'd gained in the courtyard earlier. Though she'd expended a fair amount in creating her dress, she had enough. She hoped. And if not, trying was better than admitting defeat and heading back to the dungeon.

"Stop!" she commanded.

The four men froze, only their eyes moving.

"We need to hurry," she said. "I don't think I'll be able to do that again."

The king gave her an appreciative nod and ran for the door, pulling her along behind him. The moon hung low in the sky, stars twinkling in the now clear night. The carriage waited just beyond the door. The two attached horses picked up their heads and snorted steam from their nostrils at their approach. A driver sat on the high bench up front, reins dangling loosely in his hands.

"Your highness," he offered a little bow.

"We're in a bit of a hurry. Back to the estate if you please," said the king as he opened the small door on the side of the carriage.

"Forgive me," the king said. Without further warning, he picked her up by the waist and set her inside the carriage.

Her dress seemed to fill most of the space, but he squeezed in to sit on the bench seat across from her.

Guards spilled out of the castle and surrounded the carriage.

"Your highness?" said the coachman in a wavering voice.

The king grimaced. "It seems the guards are still loyal to the queen. Do you think Gerald will get a cell next to ours?"

Amira gave the towering castle a hard look. She was not going down into that dungeon again. Ever. And the thought of the queen possibly harming Gerald or the king made her livid. She'd had enough. Far more than enough.

She threw open the door to the carriage and jumped down onto the ground. She planted her bare feet in the weak soil and closed her eyes, seeking out any help that might be nearby.

A pack of wolves heeded her silent call. They stalked the guards in the darkness. A massive stag loped into the light of the torches held by the guards. It came to stand before Amira, holding its head down low, brandishing its wide rack of horns at the now hesitant guards.

One of the guards screamed. A wolf snarled. The guards broke their line as more wolves sprang from the darkness. A black cloud descended on the scattering guards. Some of the cloud broke off, flying into the castle, revealing hundreds of bats filling the air.

"Remind me not to make you angry," said the king, now standing beside her.

Amira kept moving, one step at a time as the soil gave up what little energy it had to feed her. The stag moved with her, snorting and huffing and shaking his antlers. Once she felt strong enough, she turned to the king. "I think they will be occupied out here for now. Shall we go see about saving Gerald from the queen?"

The king eyed the carriage. He sighed and called out to the driver, "Might as well stable the horses for the night. It seems we're staying." He turned back to Amira. "Let's just hope it's in a room and not the dungeon."

The stag pawed at the ground. Amira patted its

shoulder. Three of the wolves trotted over and looked up to Amira. The bats circled overhead.

"Let's go talk to the queen," she said.

With the king by her side and the animals going before her, Amira strode into the castle.

26

ORDERS

Inside the castle, people ran from room to room. Bats flew overhead, out of reach, but causing panic all the same. When even more came in with Amira, chaos erupted. The wolves and the stag stayed close, but the bats spread out, their flapping wings putting out candles until only the wall torches were left to light the interior.

The shrill voice of the queen led Amira back to the now mostly deserted hall. Guards stood next to the prince, who was on his knees before the queen. Two of the guards stood on either side of him, their hands on his shoulders.

The courtiers who remained, stood at the back of the room watching raptly, paying little attention to the bats swooping overhead.

The wolves went in first, growling. The stag entered next, its wide antlers barely clearing the doorway. Amira followed behind him with the king.

The queen spun to face Amira, her eyes going wide. "You! You enchanted my son just like you ruined the king. This is all your fault!"

"Is it?" Amira walked further into the room, the wolves advancing before her.

The guards holding the prince started to look worried. The other two drew their swords. The stag charged forward, using its antlers to quickly disarm them. The wolves leapt at the defenseless guards, who scattered, leaving the prince alone with the queen.

"Get back here!" yelled the queen. "How dare you desert me in the face of danger. I'll see you all thrown in the dungeon for the rest of your days!"

Three of the guards circled back, but the wolves stalked them, snarling and snapping, keeping them at a distance.

The people at the back of the hall huddled together and watched raptly.

Prince Gerald got to his feet and staggered away from the queen.

Amira, with the stag beside her, came to a stop beside the prince. She pointed at the queen. "You stole me from my people. You kept me as a prisoner for eleven years. Starved me. Stole my blood until I was so weak I could barely stand. You lied about everything. And now I find that you slaughtered my people and kept others for their blood in your dungeon. Yet, I am to blame?"

The torches flared. The stag eyed the queen, tossing its sharp antlers back and forth.

"Had you let me see sunlight, let me breathe fresh air, and feel the soil under my feet, I could have helped you. Had you only asked. But instead, you took. That, in addition to all the lives you also took, I cannot forgive."

The queen looked to Prince Gerald. "Do something!"

He stood quietly by Amira's side.

Her voice rose, "You would let this monster harm your mother? Your queen?"

"You will not be harmed," said Amira. "But you will be made to understand." She turned to the prince and the king. "I mean it. See that she is kept safely for the night. I'll leave it to you as to where. Tomorrow I will bring her to the Spindelskov. You may join me or not, I also leave that to you."

With her orders given, Amira clapped her hands and turned to leave the room. The animals followed, even the bats, who swirled and swooped out of the hall. Amira left the castle with her animal escort and went to stand in the moonlight where she could clear her head and decide what exactly to do with the queen come morning.

27

HUNGRY

Amira spent most of the night walking around the castle gardens, talking to the plants and the ornamental trees. If anyone had a say in what happened to the queen, the life that had suffered around her surely did. She wasn't the only one that the queen had wronged.

When she was finally weary enough that she thought she might be able to sleep, she wandered past the entrance to the castle, thinking she might find a quiet place in the stables in the company of the animals there. A servant darted out from the castle and approached her.

For once, the servant didn't avert her eyes or mutter prayers, but addressed her directly, though somewhat shyly, much like her maids used to do in their first days in her service. "The prince has invited you to stay in the castle, if it would please you."

"Did he send you out here to look for me?"

"He did notice you were wandering in the gardens, mistress, that you hadn't left altogether."

"And the queen?"

"Confined to her room and under guard," said the servant.

A bed did sound much better than hay. "If it would not be too much trouble, I would accept his invitation."

"No trouble at all." The servant curtsied. "And for what it's worth, mistress, I'm sorry for what was done to you."

"Thank you." Amira followed the woman inside.

They went in a different direction than she'd traveled before. This time they went immediately to the left and up a short stairway. The servant opened the first door she came to.

Amira went in. A candle, half-burned down sat on a chest beside the bed. The servant picked up the pillows and fluffed them. "Prince Gerald picked this room just for you. He said you'd appreciate the morning light."

A tall, thin window graced the rounded wall. She realized the room was in the front tower of the castle, a large improvement over the dungeon. Though it wasn't as grand as the room she'd had as a child, the location and the fact that her door wouldn't be locked were more than enough to make up for it.

"If you need anything, one of us should be close by. The prince asked me to give you this." She held out an ornate bronze key."

"A key?"

"To your door. So you can lock it from the inside, should that make you feel safer." She winked.

Amira clutched the key, grateful for the control of her lock.

"Thank you."

The servant bobbed a curtsy again. "Sleep well, mistress." With that, she let herself out.

Amira stood in the middle of the room and spun around, arms outstretched, smiling. Then she noticed that the moon was already high overhead. She needed to rest. Morning would bring another set of challenges.

A nightdress like she'd worn as a child sat draped over the footboard of the bed. Knowing the gown she'd created would be uncomfortable to sleep in, she decided to change. After placing her gown carefully over the back of a chair, she climbed into the bed, surprised at how warm it was. Then she found the cloth-wrapped brick radiating heat. She'd never had the luxury of one of those before. Deciding this version of sleeping in a castle wasn't bad at all, Amira drifted off to sleep.

"Shoo!" said the maid Amira woke to find standing at the foot of her bed.

A heavy purring came from her left, quickly followed by a furry head pushing against her hand. Amira stroked the soft fur of the persuasive little beast.

"So sorry, mistress. The cat has been outside your door all morning. She slipped in when I opened the door and I haven't been able to catch her."

"She's no problem. Are you?" Amira cuddled the

purring cat.

The cat looked up at her intently. "Food?"

Excitement rushed through Amira. Finally, an animal in Katra who could speak. "You're hungry?"

"Much hungry."

Amira laughed and turned to the maid who stood unmoving with her mouth ajar. "Might she have something to eat?"

"Her job is to catch the mice in the castle, mistress. If she's hungry, she should hunt."

The cat turned to glare at the maid.

Amira ran her hands over the cat, trying to calm it. "Surely there are some kitchen scraps that could tide her over?"

She felt something moving in the belly of the cat and remembered the queen telling her of the baby moving in her stomach. "You're going to have babies?" she asked the cat.

The cat ran its head along Amira's chin, purring loudly. "Many babies. Hungry."

Amira looked to the maid.

"Yes, right away, mistress. I'll be right back with something for the cat. Would you like anything for yourself?"

Sunlight peeked through the window, falling across the bed as though it had been placed exactly just there for a reason. Either Prince Gerald was a good listener or he'd learned a good deal from his books.

"No, thank you." She dismissed the maid.

Basking in the morning sun from the comfort of her warm bed, Amira pondered the cat.

"Why can you speak but none of the other animals can?"

The cat curled onto her lap. "People talk to me and my mother before me. We remember. But it has been many cats since anyone could talk back."

"So it's not that something is wrong with the animals here, just that they have forgotten. The Spindelkin have been gone too long."

"You're here now." The cat closed its eyes and its breathing slowed.

The cat woke up immediately when the maid returned a short time later, a plate of kitchen scraps in her hand. It jumped off the bed and padded silently over to the plate.

"The prince and king have asked after you, mistress." The maid gave the gown on the end of the bed a meaningful look. "If you would like something less grand, I'm sure I could find a dress for you."

"This will do, thank you."

"Will you be needing help with your hair?" asked the maid.

Amira did miss her maids brushing her hair. When she'd been in the Spindelskov, she hadn't given her hair much thought at all. The trees and animals didn't care about such things.

"That would be nice, thank you."

The maid nodded, inviting Amira to sit on the stool

near a table with a pitcher of water and a bowl. In her nightdress, she sat quietly while the maid began to work on her hair.

"My goodness, there are little bits of twigs all through this. Who did your hair last?"

Amira giggled, not caring if the maid believed her or not. "Birds."

"You think I'm simple... Oh, yes, I suppose if you can speak to the cats, and after what you did last night, birds aren't much of a stretch, are they?"

The maid clucked her tongue as the pile of tiny twigs and dried blossoms grew on the table. "I suppose I should see about taking lessons from the birds then," she said after a while. "Twigs make good hairpins. The birds did a very nice job."

"I'll tell them you said so."

"That should do it," said the maid after a while. "Can't say as I've done the hair of a Spindelkin before, but I hope you'll approve."

Amira delicately patted her hair, exploring the simple twisted bun the maid had styled. Though she preferred her hair down, now that she'd had time with that in the forest, she supposed this was more in keeping with what the ladies in the castle expected. After the night before, fitting in, even just a little would probably be in her favor.

"Very nice, thank you," she said.

"Oh good. I'll leave you to get dressed. Unless you need help?"

"I can manage."

The maid gratefully scurried out of the room. Amira wondered if she expected her to have a tail or some other strange thing hidden under her nightdress.

The cat wound around Amira's legs and then went to the door and sat down, tail flicking back and forth. Amira quickly changed.

Even though she knew the door was unlocked and that she held the key, her heart fluttered to find she could come and go of her own accord. As soon as she had the door open, the cat ran out. Amira followed, wondering where she might find the king and the prince.

TRUCE

Amira walked down the little flight of stairs and followed the sound of raised voices to a room across from the great hall. The door was closed and a guard stood outside. He took one look at her approaching and knocked on the door.

"The kin woman is here, your highness."

"You keep that monster away from me," said the queen.

"Show her in," called Prince Gerald.

The guard shrugged and held the door open for Amira. "You might want those wolves of yours before you go in," the guard whispered.

"They're asleep now, but thank you for the warning," said Amira.

The three of them were seated at a round table. The remains of a meal sat in the middle. The queen's plate was mostly untouched. There were no other chairs.

"Good morning, Amira," said the king.

"Is it?" She had the distinct feeling nothing would be good until the queen was dealt with.

Prince Gerald stood and offered her his seat.

The thought of sharing a table with the queen made her skin crawl. "I'm fine standing, thank you."

Prince Gerald nodded and returned to his seat.

The king turned his chair so he could face Amira. "We addressed the advisory council this morning. They have a proposal. I hope you will hear us out."

He looked nervous and that made her nervous. She regretted not taking the offered chair.

"What is this proposal?" she asked.

The king looked to the prince, giving him a tight nod.

Prince Gerald cleared his throat. "In the interest of healing our land—"

"Don't you dare say it," said the queen. "I forbid any such thing."

Prince Gerald cast a glare in her direction without quite turning all the way around. "It's your fault and the fault of our ancestors that we're in this mess. The council has agreed to strip you of your power, which means you no longer have the ability to forbid anything, Mother." He spit the last word out as though it were distasteful.

"What mess is this exactly?" asked Amira, not sure if she really wanted to know as it seemed to involve her.

The Prince turned his full attention to Amira. "As I was saying, the advisory council suggested that the best way to heal our land was to heal the rift between our people. And to ask for your help," he half glared at his mother again, "though we truly don't deserve it."

"Perhaps not," said Amira. "But the kin will always do their part to heal and care for the land. It is what we do, what we were created for."

The king nodded. "We have agreed to let your people into Katra. Though I have concerns about their safety given this truce we are proposing."

"Perhaps, rather than your guards hunting the Spindelkin, they could protect them?" Amira suggested.

"It will take some time to make sure all the guards understand the truce, but yes, that is a reasonable request," said Prince Gerald.

"Good," said Amira. "I will need to get word to my people. It will also take time to make them understand this truce." She considered how to make them trust the people of Katra. "They will need evidence that you have accepted us after all this time."

Prince Gerald cast a worried glance at the king.

"The queen must pay for what she has done," said Amira. "She will come to the Spindelskov to face the elders. They will pass judgment, not me. Secondly, you will free any of my former maids who remain in the dungeon."

The queen truly looked worried then. "They'll spread rumors."

"They aren't rumors, Mother," said the Prince. "You did keep a kin girl in the dungeon for eleven years and used her blood to temporarily heal our land. That is the truth of it."

Prince Gerald turned to Amira. "I would ask that no harm comes to my mother."

Amira's brows rose. "After all she's done? After all the lives she's taken and those she's ruined?" She shook her head. "I can't promise anything, but you are welcome to travel with us and speak to the elders on her behalf."

"Go on," said the king. "I'll meet with the guards and see to freeing any maids in the dungeons. And remember what I said to the council. I'm holding you to that."

Prince Gerald nodded. "We best be on our way then. I'd like to get this resolved as soon as possible."

The king stood. "I'll have horses readied for you and send guards along to ensure your safety."

"They may travel with us until we reach the Spindelskov," Amira decreed. "They will need to wait for us at the edge of the forest."

The king looked as though he might argue but after a long moment, he nodded. He got up and left the room.

"Can you ride a horse?" asked Prince Gerald.

"I suppose if I can ride on an elk, I can manage. It will allow me to teach your animals how to speak again. In the absence of Spindelkin, they've forgotten."

"Yet another thing we've lost," said the prince.

The queen stood. "Are you going to let this slip of a forest sprite dictate our future?"

"You've ruined enough, Mother. The future deserves a better chance." He stood up stiffly, his words just as tight. "I need to pack. Amira, would you please wait for us by the stables?"

Not sure what to make of his request and posture or the angry looks passing between mother and son, Amira left them and went outside in the blessed sunshine to wait.

29

THE SPREAD

Guards emerged from the castle one by one until there were six of them. One was still yawning as he came to stand near Amira. She recognized one of them as the guard who had been by the door of the room where she'd just met with the royal family.

"Taking Katra by storm, aren't you?" he remarked.

"I don't know as I hold any control over the weather." But as she said that, she recalled the sky growing dark when she'd been younger and in the courtyard for the first time. Maybe she had more to learn about the Spindelkin just as the people of Katra did.

"The legends say you do," he said.

"I suppose I shall have to read these legends of yours." If she learned to read, yet another thing that had been kept from her.

Two stable boys hurried out with two large horses and set to attaching them to a cart. She imagined it was much like the cart that had taken her from the tower. Another man came out of the stable to drive the cart around the side of the castle. Before she could wonder further what that was about, the prince emerged from the castle with the queen. Three servants followed behind, their arms full of wrapped bundles. Two more guards escorted the queen.

The stable boys who had taken care of the cart, now led more horses out of the stables, transferring the reins to each of the guards. They brought a pair out to the prince and queen until everyone was mounted on a horse but Amira. The horses pulling the cart came back into view, joining the waiting herd in the yard. In the back of the cart sat a jumble of women blinking hard in the bright morning light.

The prince brought his horse alongside Amira. "We have released half of the maids from the dungeon." He pointed to the cart. "The other half will be released upon my safe return."

She looked up at him, so high above her on horseback. "Do you truly think I would harm you?"

A slow smile spread across his lips. "No, I don't think so. But my parents..." He shrugged. "They wish me to be careful and safe."

"Thank you for releasing them. You should see that they are returned to their homes. They did nothing wrong and have been kept here so long. I'm sure your family will find a way to make that up to them?" She suggested with a stern look that she'd learned from the queen.

"Yes, of course." Prince Gerald rode over to the men driving the cart and talked with them and then returned. "They will be taken care of," he assured her.

There were no other horses waiting for riders. "Am I to ride with you?"

"If you'd like." Prince Gerald turned to look at the queen and then the guards around them. "Some say you have enchanted me."

"Have I?"

He chuckled. "Yes, but not in the way they think." He held out his hand. "Come on then. We might as well light off some more rumors while we're at it."

She took his hand, holding tight as he lifted her onto the horse. With her legs hanging off one side, she sat sideways in front of him. It was a long way down and with everyone else appearing to know exactly what they were doing on horseback, she was grateful that Prince Gerald hadn't expected her to fit right in.

The horse moved with a much smoother gait than the elk had. The prince sitting right behind her also made the ride more enjoyable. He smelled much better than either the elk or horse and he pointed out buildings as they passed by, explaining what they were and who lived there.

When he wasn't talking, she petted the horse and talked to it, getting to know the beast a little. While it didn't talk back, it did seem to enjoy her company.

"I think he likes you," said the prince.

"I'm going to need a lot of help with the animals," she mused, seeing the fields dotted with cattle, pigs, and sheep.

"We're not expecting an immediate recovery," assured the prince.

Amira nodded, noting the gardens by the cottages they passed now that they were beyond the city. Soon they came to fields tended by people in worn clothing. Children carried buckets and picked crops beside their parents.

For the next three days, they traveled the road in a much more comfortable manner than her trip through Katra chained in the wagon. They slept in tents along the roadside and ate as they traveled. Whenever they came to a cottage near the road, Amira asked to stop to spend a few minutes with their gardens or animals. The queen complained about each delay. Prince Gerald made sure she was comfortable and taken care of but otherwise ignored her, spending most of his time with Amira.

They traveled beyond the fields and finally Amira could see the tower in the distance. Tiny figures moved about the tower, on the ground and up on the top.

"Did you build this before or after the war with the Spindelkin?"

"It was under construction when your people emerged from the forest. My mother ordered it built when you left. She was sure the Spindelkin would attack. And they did."

"And you defeated them with iron like when you

captured me?"

He bowed his head. "I'm sorry about that. Will you forgive me?"

She quite enjoyed his bashful look. "I'm working on it."

He nodded.

"From where the trees stand now, I gather my kin didn't get very far from the forest. You must have had a force here ready for them?"

"We had guards here with the workers. They spotted movement in the trees and acted quickly." He paused. "How does the position of the trees tell you this?"

"When we die, a tree sprouts so that we live on in that form." Her voice grew quiet as she remembered those that had died in the dungeons, away from the sun and earth. "When we have no light or soil, it seems we turn to dust and vanish from the world forever."

The prince grimaced. "I'm sorry, Amira. We didn't know."

"Neither did I. About either one. Your mother kept all knowledge of my people from me. All I knew was a few hints from the stories your father read to me."

"Wait, are you saying you can't read on your own?"

"They did not leave books with me and no one taught me how."

His hands were busy holding the horse and helping her keep her balance, but he put his chin on her shoulder for a moment. His beard was soft against her skin. "I am also sorry for that too. I could teach you, if you'd like?"

She liked that idea very much but surely he was busy. "I'm sure you have much more important things to do."

"In the name of righting the wrongs of the past, this is also an important thing to do. Besides," he said with a smile. "I would like to spend more time with you."

She wondered if he would feel that same way once the elders passed their judgment on his mother. She hoped so.

When they reached the tower, the queen announced that she was hungry. The guards didn't argue. They busied themselves with unloading supplies and carried them inside.

Prince Gerald slid off the horse and held out his hands to help Amira down. She smiled as he held her by the waist and lifted her off the horse to deposit her on the ground.

"What do you think the Spindelkin will do with my mother?" Prince Gerald asked quietly.

Amira hadn't been among her own kind very long, but she knew one thing for sure. "Spindelkin don't keep prisoners. We have no dungeons."

Though, the trees could eat people, merge with them, as the tree had been trying to do with the elders she'd rescued. Would the elders demand that of the queen? She glanced at Prince Gerald and hoped not.

He was looking at the tower where the others were sitting on the grass around the base, enjoying a meal. She gave him a little push. "Go on and eat."

He nodded gratefully and went to join the others.

Amira sat in the grass, lifting her face to the sun, enjoying the quiet. She'd been used to only having a visitor or two at a time in her dungeon bedroom, and had spent more of her time alone in the Spindelskov. A few minutes without complaints from the queen or continuous conversation passing between the guards as they rode was a welcome break.

Once she saw that the others had finished their meal she walked over to them. "Gather your mother and let's be on our way."

Amira didn't wait to make sure the prince agreed. She started off for the forest herself, knowing that with his long legs and even with the queen in tow, he'd catch up quickly.

What she did not expect were the distant shadowy figures she spotted at the edge of the forest. She reached out to touch the nearest tree.

"What is happening?" she asked.

"We have told the others of your coming. We saw you a long way off," said the tree.

Whether the kin were friendly or would honor the truce she was going to propose remained to be seen. The only way she'd know was to talk to them. She glanced over her shoulder to see Prince Gerald talking to the guards, his mother at his side. They appeared to be arguing. Amira left them to it and strode toward the forest.

30

Judgment

She reached the waiting kin long before Prince Gerald and his uncooperative mother caught up to her. But at least they were heading in her direction.

A hunched figure stepped out of the treeline. "You are the one called Amira?" he asked.

She nodded.

"What is this I hear of peace?"

Amira explained the truce the prince and the king had proposed. "And they offer the queen to us for judgment," she said.

The elderly kin chewed his lips as he watched the royal mother and son walking towards the Spindelskov. "It is not our place to judge humans, Amira."

"Then let the trees judge."

"They do not bother themselves with the dealings of men."

Amira thought of all the terrible things the queen

had done. "You can't mean to say that she should go free?"

The elder gave her a long look. "Do you think she should go free?"

"Definitely not."

"Then, since you are the only one of us who has experience in the ways of men, it is for you to pass judgment."

Amira went cold. In talking to the plants and trees around the castle, they'd all been displeased with the queen and the lack of Spindelkin. Yet, none of them had suggested punishment. Maybe she should ask some of the trees from the spread. They might be more helpful.

"I will think on the matter of the queen. But as to peace?"

"Those that sought war now surround us." He pointed at the trees of the spread. "We are few and the needs of the land are many. We need peace. To grow our numbers once more, to serve all those that need us as best we can." He nodded. "We are agreeable to peace. Will they grant safe passage to Spindelkin?"

Prince Gerald arrived at her side, towing his mother along by the arm. "Yes, we will offer safe passage," he stated. "What is to be done with my mother?"

Amira noted the fine sheen of sweat on his brow and the tightness in his voice. "It seems I will be the one dealing with your mother."

"You?" His brows rose.

Amira addressed the kin in the trees behind the

elder. "May I borrow a couple of you to watch this woman so that the prince and the elder can work out an accord?"

Three kin came forward, carrying spears in their hands. The queen shrank back.

"Come, let us walk among the new trees for a while," she said to the kin and the queen. "I will hear their counsel."

The three kin stepped toward the queen. She backed against Prince Gerald.

"You don't plan to leave me to these...things, do you?"

He scowled. "Maybe if you hadn't stolen Amira from her people and hurt so many others, you wouldn't need to ask that question."

The Spindelkin pointed their spears at her.

"Gerald, please. You can't do this to me," she shrieked, grabbing his arm.

He pried her hand off of him. "I think I'm done with the name that you gave me. I prefer the one Amira gave me: Corvin. Remember him? The son you left to die?"

The queen spun around, but the Spindelkin were on all sides, blocking her escape.

The elder peered up at the prince. "Corvin? That is you?"

"That is the name Amira gave me as an infant," he said uncertainly.

The elder rubbed his bearded chin. "I have learned the names of all Spindelkin. Corvin was one of us, but you do not appear to be of the kin. We lost all sense of him long ago."

"I was born part Spindelkin because of my mother. Amira made me human. Wait, except for one thing." He pulled out his dagger and sawed at his bearded cheek. The prince turned his exposed patch of golden scales to the elder.

The elder grinned, holding out his hands, taking the prince's in his own. "Welcome back, Corvin of Katra."

"I don't know as these scales make me one of you."

"Nonsense," said the elder. "Amira may have the gift to make you appear as one of your own, but your heart will always be ours. No other reason why a man of Katra would seek peace with Spindelkin."

The prince's gaze met Amira's. "Oh, I don't know about that."

Amira blushed.

"Perhaps your heart belongs to *one* of ours," the elder said with a wink. "Amid all the tragedy caused by the queen, there is also good to be found."

The queen made a disgusted sound. Amira turned to her, all hint of her smile gone. "My birth mother was among the fallen. How about we go walk among the trees here and find her? I'm sure she would like to speak to you."

The queen paled. "But they are just trees."

"They speak and they remember. You may not be able to speak to them—"

The elder held up his hand. "I can help with that. If I may borrow your dagger?" He nodded toward the prince's belt.

The prince unsheathed his dagger and held it out to the elder.

The elder poked the tip of his finger. A golden drop of blood welled up. Before the queen could react, he dabbed the droplet on her forehead.

"Now you will understand."

The queen wailed. "You've turned me into a monster!"

Amira shook her head. "You already were." She tapped her chin. "Fully understanding the Spindelkin and what you have done to your land, that will be your punishment. We will visit each tree in the spread, you and I, and you will hear their stories and learn from them. While we do that, you will live with the women you changed so you will also understand what you have done to them. When we have finished, I will leave it to you to decide whether you wish to return to the castle or not."

The queen drew herself up, staring down her nose at Amira with a scowl firmly lodged on her face. "That won't take long. Of course I'll go back to the castle, and I'll make sure you never set foot there again."

Amira shrugged. "We will see. Let's begin."

She started for the nearest tree. The three armed Spindelkin drove the queen after Amira.

"I'll join you shortly," said the prince. "I have a few questions for the elder."

Amira nodded.

When they reached the first tree, Amira grabbed

the queen's hand and pressed it to the smooth bark of the long trunk. She pressed her other hand to the tree as well so they could both hear.

The tree breathed a long sigh. Its leaves shivered. "Little Amira, all grown," it said.

The queen gasped. "It talked."

"They are alive. Now think of all the trees you had cut down."

"We needed lumber."

"Then you harvest trees outside of Spindelkin land."

"But they were trees of Katra," said the queen.

"Katra was Spindelkin land long before you came here. But did you ask? No, you took."

The queen shook her head. "It wasn't me. My ancestors did that long ago."

"And you continue their practice," said the tree, full of accusation.

"But we needed land for fields, so the animals could graze," she said.

"Excuses," said the tree.

"Tell us of your life," said Amira, "so the queen can understand what we are."

The tree spent hours talking to the queen. When Amira came back to herself, the sun had begun to set.

The queen didn't say a word.

"Are you hungry?" Amira asked.

"I suppose so," the queen said quietly. She looked around, blinking. "Where did the others go?"

"They left once you connected with the tree."

"And Gerald, or Corvin, or whatever he's calling himself today?"

"They went back to the tower, I think." She started back toward the tower herself. "Come, you will need to eat and rest. We will have another conversation with a tree tomorrow."

The queen looked around at the vast tree-studded field. "You're going to make me talk to every one of these trees?"

"Every one, yes."

"Aren't you hungry?" she asked.

"I don't eat food, not like you." Amira waved her hand at the sky and field. "All of this sustains me."

"But you ate food when you were a child."

"Only because I didn't have what I really needed. You starved me."

"No wonder you were so small and weak," the queen said.

"You knew this. Don't pretend otherwise," Amira snapped.

The queen looked away.

They walked back to the tower without speaking. Amira left the queen with one of the guards at the door and went to sit out in the quiet and peace of the grass.

Footsteps behind her made her turn around.

The prince stood there looking down at her with a smile. "Are you going to stay out here all night?"

"I haven't decided. My thoughts on the tower aren't all that favorable."

He sat down beside her. "That's understandable."

She turned to face him. "Are you really changing your name?"

"Yes. Gerald never felt right, but Corvin does. It's like the difference between wearing someone else's clothing and your own." He glanced at her dress made of leaves. "If that makes any sense to you?"

"I think I understand, yes."

He fiddled with three blades of grass, braiding them together. "I wanted to thank you for your decisions regarding my mother. Even with all the awful things she did, I didn't want to see her hurt."

"We aren't the monsters she thinks we are," she said stiffly.

"Clearly not. You were right in what you said earlier. We are all trying to be better. I hope that she will too."

Amira nodded.

The sky took on a rosy glow as the sun sunk toward the horizon. The evening bugs chirped in the grass and a bat darted overhead.

Prince Corvin coughed nervously. "I wanted to ask if you would consider staying at the tower with me. In your own room, of course. While you are dealing with my mother." He gave her a hopeful look. "And maybe after?"

"Don't you need to return to the castle?"

"I was thinking... What I mean to say is one of the things I asked the elder, is if the Spindelkin would mind if I built a home here, incorporating the tower."

"A second castle?"

"Perhaps not so grand as that, but a place you would be comfortable. One where any Spindelkin would be welcome. It will take time to get our people used to one another and there's so much work to do with repairing the land. I thought it would be nice to have a neutral place here, close to the Spindelskov rather than in the heart of Katra."

She raised her eyebrow. "And I would be staying here?"

He did one of those nervous coughs again. "My father has insisted, against my mother's wishes, as you might imagine, that I make the proposal to join our people together official."

"What exactly are you *proposing*?"

He took her hand again, rubbing his thumb over her thin fingers. "Marriage?"

Amira's heart leapt into her throat. The queen had always told her that if she were to marry, it would be for the benefit of Katra, that's what a good princess did. But she'd never expected to live long enough for a marriage to happen. That a wedding might be in her future was exciting but also made her very nervous.

"I'm not opposed to marrying you, but it's very sudden."

"The elder has given his approval. But yes, I agree," he said.

"You got the elder's approval?"

He nodded.

"Aren't you supposed to marry a princess? I'm not one."

"My mother said both of those same things. My father argued that the Spindelkin don't abide by royalty and so you, being their chosen delegate to Katra—"

"I am?"

He grinned. "According to me and the elder, yes. Being the chosen delegate entitles you to the same status. So yes, a marriage between us would unite the Spindelkin and the people of Katra."

"So only a political marriage," she stated, looking at his hand on hers.

"I'd like it to be more. In time. I'll talk to my father and ask him for a year to plan our wedding. It will take time to build a home here. We can work on that together so you can make it how you would like it. We can learn more about each other too."

Amira squeezed his hand. "Then yes, I would like that very much, Corvin."

He grinned. "There is one other thing," he said, his face only inches from hers.

"I would like that too." Not bothering to wait for him, Amira closed the distance and enjoyed her first kiss.

They sat together in the grass, watching the stars shine in the darkening sky as the last wisps of red sun sunk below the horizon.

EPILOGUE

Amira tapped the queen on the shoulder where she stood by the towering tree. "That was the last one. Shall we go home?"

"I'd like to stay a little while longer, if you don't mind." The queen sat in the grass, tucking her simple brown skirt around her legs. Her bare toes wiggled in the dirt just like Amira's. She wore her hair in a thick braid that hung down to her waist, grey streaking the dark strands.

"It's so quiet here, isn't it?" the queen asked.

Amira nodded. "Do you like it better here than the house?"

The queen laughed. "I don't know why you insist on calling it that. It's a castle, maybe a small one, but the title still fits."

"A castle has a dungeon. My house never will."

The queen bowed her head. "Amira, I'm truly sorry about keeping you in the dungeon. And all the rest of it. It was wrong of me. I understand that now."

Amira smiled and nodded. Though the queen had

apologized similarly before, it was hard to know if she meant it or was just saying what she thought she was supposed to say in order to be set free. There was only one way to find out, and now that they'd spoken with every tree in the spread, it was time.

"Then your punishment is over. It's too late to set out now, but if you wish to return to the castle tomorrow, I'll have a carriage readied for you."

The queen took a long look at the Spindelskov in the distance and the trees and flowers in the field, and then to the large estate that Corvin had built. The stone tower stood on one corner. Animals, no longer confined to the lower level of the tower, wandered freely, knowing to go into their shelters at night now that Amira and the other kin had been working with them. Fields of abundant crops grew on the other side of the estate, stretching across the land between their home and the city of Katra.

Her gaze fell on Amira's swelling belly. "I think the king has Katra well enough in hand and he has little love for me these days. If you wouldn't mind, I'd like to stay here."

Amira did her best to keep her jaw from gaping. "You don't wish to take your place at the castle?"

"My days as queen are over," she shook her head sadly. "The waving fists and angry chants when I arrived at your wedding made the people's opinion clear. I hope, when the day comes, you'll be a much better queen than I was." She patted Amira's arm. "You already are."

Amira's heart swelled to hear sincere, kind words

from the queen. "Thank you."

"I'm sure you'll be a better mother too," she said. "Perhaps I could focus on being a grandmother instead of a queen. Your mother might be a tree these days, but we've come to an understanding, or we're working on it, anyway," she said quietly. "We both have regrets as mothers and would like to make sure you have none now that it is your turn."

Amira bit her lower lip. "The elder said our child has an equal chance of being human or kin. You do realize that? That your grandchild could be like Corvin was at birth? A monster?"

The queen cringed. "I would not use that word again, given the chance. If you'll give me that chance?"

"Your son would like that very much," said Amira.

"And you?"

The queen would never be her mother and too many horrible things had happened between them to be friends, but if the queen could learn to accept the Spindelkin, Amira supposed she could do the same for the woman.

Amira nodded. "If we are no longer addressing you as queen, what name should I use?"

"No one has used my name but the king and my own mother, but you may call me Meg."

No longer having to think of the woman before her as queen, helped put some of who she had been aside. Meg wasn't a lofty woman in a fancy gown with a shrill voice and high expectations. The woman before her was one that she hoped, one day, she might come to like. But for now, she would give her a chance.

"Yes, Meg, I would be happy to have a grandmother to help raise our child."

Meg smiled and stood, holding out her hand. "Then let's get you up and back to the house before Corvin sends out the guard to look for us."

Amira took Meg's hand. Together, they walked through what would someday be the new edge of the Spindelskov to their home where their people were learning a little more each day, how to live as one.

About the Author

Jean Davis writes an array of speculative fiction and plays with chickens. When not ruining fictional lives from the comfort of her writing chair, she can be found devouring books and sushi, weeding her flower garden, or picking up hundreds of sticks while attempting to avoid the abundant snake population that also shares her yard. She lives in West Michigan with her musical husband, an attention-craving terrier, and a small flock of chickens and ducks.

Read her blog, and sign up for her mailing list at www.jeandavisauthor.com. You'll also find her on Facebook and Instagram at JeanDavisAuthor, and on Goodreads and Amazon.

If you enjoyed this book, please consider leaving a review. They are much appreciated. Thank you!